her
DESTINY

her DESTINY

Monica Murphy

Her Destiny

everafter ROMANCE

Chapter
ONE

The Future

I met a boy.
And I fell for him.
Hard.
He was sweet, he was kind and no matter how much he tried to deny me…
He couldn't resist.
And neither could I.
He was my first kiss.
The first boy I let touch me.
He was my first…everything.
But he walked away from me.
To protect me…from himself.
When the only protection I really wanted…
The only protection I needed…
Was him.
When he walked back into my life.
So unexpectedly.
I was mad.
I was happy.

I pushed him away.
But he wouldn't go.
It didn't matter what I did.
What I said.
How I treated him.
I couldn't deny his love for me.
Or my love for him.
And now I know he was the one for me.
He was my…
Destiny.

Chapter
TWO

September 2nd

Dear Diary,
Oh, screw it. Let's start this off the way I really want to:
Dear Nick,
Why? That's the word, the question that runs through my head whenever I think of you. Why did you leave me? Why did you not want to see me? Why did you tell me you loved me and then never attempted to see me again?

I don't understand.

It doesn't help that I'm a little drunk. A little frustrated. Drowning my sorrows with alcohol, I've turned into my mother and I haven't even graduated high school yet.

I'm a mess. Over you. It hurts so much, your rejection. Why?

See...I'm back to that word. Why. It's the dumbest word in existence because it doesn't help anything. You don't help anything. You don't help me.

You left me. You didn't want me. No one wants me. Poor stupid little Reverie, believing in love and truth and family—I'm left disappointed. The only one who really takes care of me is the last person who I thought cared and that's my brother. But then again, if I can't count on my brother, then who can I count on?

Certainly not you, Nick.

Why?

Don't answer that. I don't want to know. The truth hurts. I'd rather live in my little bubble and pretend I never knew you.

But I can't. You haunt my thoughts. I went to a party. I drank tonight to escape you. I kissed another boy to escape you and all his lips and wandering hands managed to do was make me miss you.

I hate you.

I love you.

Love,

Reverie

Chapter
THREE

September 16th

Dear Reverie,
I know you won't get this email. I'm writing it on my phone and saving it in the drafts folder because I don't even have your email address. I tried texting you and I know the messages were delivered but you didn't reply. Did they take your phone away? Or are you just ignoring me?

I deserve to be ignored. I ignored you, which was stupid but I thought it was for the best. They put me in jail. Again. They could only hold me there for a few hours though. They have nothing on me in regards to Krista's death because I didn't do it. You already know this because you were with me that night. Not that I told them. I wasn't about to put you into a bad situation. How could you explain why you were with me to your parents? I know they'd freak out and the last thing you want to do is disappoint them.

You know I was frustrated with Krista and the things she did to us. To me. To you. Yeah, I didn't like her much but I definitely didn't want her dead. I feel terrible about that. They still don't know who did it. They suspect her dad but they can't hold him either. There was evidence showing she had sex with someone but it was contaminated.

Ruined.

They have no idea who she was with that night but I know for sure it wasn't me. And you know it too.

I still think about that night, at what had started out as one of the best nights of my life before it spiraled out of control and turned into a nightmare. You're my alibi but I kept that to myself. No way did I want you to risk your relationship with your parents. I know they mean a lot to you. Family is important. I miss my mom every single day and wish she were still with me.

But wishes are for fools.

I miss you too. You have no idea how much. I hate that the last time I saw you, you were walking into your parents' house, your back to me, thinking everything was going to be okay. I wish I could go back in time and really make everything okay, you know? But there I go again, wishing for things that can never happen. That'll get me nowhere.

I heard about your dad and I'm sorry. I don't know what's truth and what are lies but I know it must hurt to have such horrible things said about your parents. You're in school now—are they treating you okay? How's Evan reacting to all of this? Your mom? I heard from Michael and Heather that your family packed up and left within twenty-four hours of my dropping you off at your house.

Considering I was still being held at the jail when that happened, I had no idea. I missed out on telling you goodbye and I regret that more than anything.

I'll probably never see you again. But just know this—this summer was the best time of my life. Being with you, falling in love with you, was like nothing I ever experienced before. I wish I could talk to you. See your smile. Hear your laugh. Hold you in my arms. Kiss your sweet lips.

I want it all.

But I can't have you.

So I'll wait for you to come to me in my dreams.

Love, Nick

Chapter
FOUR

September 30th

"**C**ome on," he murmurs against my lips, his voice low and persuasive. "You gotta give me a little something."

I've given this guy way more than I should have already. I can't believe I'm even doing this but I drank too much tonight. Partied a little too much, which has become my new norm no matter how much I secretly hate it. I have new friends. A new attitude. Good girl Reverie Hale doesn't exist anymore.

She's gone. Wiped from existence.

He had his eyes on me all night and I finally gave in and talked to him. Smiled and flirted with him. Let him drag me into a dark bedroom where he tugged me down so we were both sitting on the edge of the mattress. His hand in my hair, his mouth locked with mine, kissing me so thoroughly my jaw is sore.

"Haven't I given you enough?" I say after I push him away. I'm breathing hard and so is he. He's tall and broad shouldered and he tastes of beer. In the dark I can almost pretend he's someone else, which is counterproductive because I'm trying to erase a certain someone from my brain, not pretend that certain someone is still in my life.

"Not nearly enough." He lunges for me and I squeal when he takes me down so I'm lying on my back on the bed and he's hovering above me, his shoulders blocking out most of the light, though it's pretty dark in here to begin with.

I don't even know his name.

Splaying my hands, I smack them against his chest, preventing him from kissing me again. "I should go," I tell him solemnly, my gaze direct. My friends are downstairs waiting for me. Maybe. I saw Rachel had paired off with a guy and I don't know about Talia. I need to find them and get out of here.

"You're not going anywhere," he says with a wicked smile, leaning in to steal a kiss.

I let him, trying my best to lose myself in the softness of his lips, the quickness of his tongue. He's a decent kisser. I've gone from never been kissed to being kissed far too much in a shockingly short amount of time. I'm trying to shed the old me.

The me I didn't like. The me who was sheltered and stupid and so naïve it's almost embarrassing. I look back at those silly, childish journal entries and cringe in embarrassment. I was such a baby then.

When his hands touch my breasts I jerk away from his mouth and out of his hold, my entire body going cold. I may kiss many guys and pretend I like them but the minute they touch me below the neck, forget it. It's like I shut down.

I can't handle them touching me. It brings back too many memories. Memories of my short time with Nick. How sweet he was. How foolish I am now to still think of him.

All thoughts of Nicholas Fairfield are a waste of my time since he clearly doesn't want me. Or love me.

Standing, I run a hand over my hair and tug at the hem of my sweater. "I really need to go."

"Why?"

"I need to find my friends." It sounds like an excuse. And my friends probably don't give a crap what I'm doing. We've only hung out together for the last month and a half or so. It's amazing how much I've done in that short amount of time.

I don't know whether I should be ashamed or proud.

"Your friends are fine." He reaches for me, his hand swiping at air as I leap away from him. This one is persistent, more than the previous ones. "Come on, stay with me." He's trying to sound coaxing but all I hear is the whiny tinge to his voice.

"See ya." I flee the bedroom before he can say another word, before he can try and reach out and grab me again. I don't want him near me. I don't want anyone near me.

I rush down the stairs, the loud music throbbing through my body, in my head. I spot Talia talking with a tall, dark-skinned boy with long black hair. He's gorgeous and I can tell she thinks so too, what with the enraptured look on her face as she listens to him.

"Tally." I stop beside her and flash a quick smile in the dark-haired boy's direction. He stops speaking, staring at me like I just ruined his game, which I probably did. "You ready to go?"

"Not really," she says, giving a side jerk of her head toward the guy. "We were talking, Justice and I."

"Justice?" I turn to him. "Interesting name."

"That's what everyone says," he mutters, looking irritated.

I reach out and touch his arm, marveling at how smooth and warm his skin is. "I have a weird name too."

"What is it?" He drops his gaze, looking at my very pale hand against his dark skin before he lifts his head and stares at me.

Oh. I wish I would've met him before the other guy. I have a feeling this one is a lot more interesting. "Reverie." I drop my hand away from his arm when I see the way Tally is glaring at me.

He frowns. "As in Reverie Hale?"

Crap. Everyone knows about me, not that I want them to. My family's scandal has been all over the media and though I've gone into semi-hiding by moving into Evan's apartment, I've been able to move in plain sight for the most part.

"I knew I recognized you," Justice continues, a big grin on his face. He points at me and backs away a few steps. "How's your holy roller dad huh? Spending all that money he stole?"

His voice is loud and drawing other people's attention. The party goes quiet. I swear even the music fades and I'm left standing there staring at him, Tally watching everything go down, her mouth hanging open. She's not rushing to my defense or telling Justice to shut up. No one is.

I'm all alone but what else is new?

"Did your daddy buy you this necklace with stolen money?" He strides toward me, reaching out to grab hold of the delicate chain that's around my neck. A necklace with a simple gold locket that Mother gave me a long time ago, that once belonged to my grandma. Justice's fingers curl around the fragile gold and I try to jerk out of his touch.

Instead I rear back so quickly the necklace breaks and I gasp, watching as the old locket falls to the floor. I dip down to grab it but Justice is faster, bending over and sweeping the locket into his palm.

"Give that back," I say, my voice shaky, holding out my hand. My fingers tremble and I curl them inward, hating the sign of weakness. "It's mine."

"You want it?" He dangles it from his fingers, the smirk on his face ugly. Mocking. "Come and get it."

I stare at him, contemplating what I should do, what I should say. Tally is gone. It's like the going got tough and she took off. I have no idea where Rachel is. She's the loosest of my two new friends. She's probably naked in a stranger's bed somewhere upstairs.

"It was my grandmother's," I tell him, trying one last time to gain… what? Sympathy? We've drawn a crowd. Glancing around, I see the anger on all their faces. I don't know any of them. I'm at some random party that's far from where I usually hang out. I go to private school and when I first arrived for my senior year, I shunned my old friends. Found new ones that I thought would fit better with my new lifestyle.

Now I wished for those old friends. At least they're loyal. I wouldn't even be at this stupid party with people I didn't know if I'd stayed with them. Vanessa and Valerie. We were silly together. We called ourselves the "V" girls because we all have Vs in our names and we were virgins. Stupid.

I'm not a virgin anymore. I don't even belong with the "V" girls.

I don't know who I belong with.

"You're a liar," Justice practically snarls, throwing the locket at my face. It bounces off my cheek and I reach up, hold my hand against my face as I bend down and grab the locket from where it landed by my feet. "Get the fuck out of here."

I scurry out of the house without another word, not once looking back as the tears stream down my cheeks, the locket still clutched in my hand. I walk blindly down the street and grab my cell phone out of the back pocket of my jeans, hitting speed dial and hoping like crazy Evan answers. It's late and he's probably with a girl.

He's always with a girl.

"It's midnight," he growls when he answers. I swear I hear a female's voice in the background. I'm sure I do. My brother has gone hog wild lately.

So have I so I guess we're just rebelling against the crap that's been thrown at us.

"I need you to come get me," I say, stopping as I glance around the street. The homes are nice, the neighborhood older. I rode over with Rachel and Tally and I really don't want to find them and ask them to take me home. I don't even think they would. They're too wrapped up in their own stuff and Tally ran as fast as she could when the argument started. I bet she's mad that I blew her chance with that jerk named Justice.

Stupid name. Stupid guy. Stupid new friends.

The heavy sigh that I hear tells me Evan isn't pleased. That makes two of us. "Where are you?" he grumbles.

"I'll text you the address. Plug it into your GPS." I pause, hating how vulnerable I feel, how vulnerable I sound. "Please, Evan. Hurry."

"I'll get there as soon as I can." He ends the call before I can say another word and I practically collapse onto the sidewalk, sitting on the edge as I type in the address and text it to Evan.

This is my life now. It's done a complete one-eighty from a year ago. Heck, six months ago. I started the summer innocent and hopeful. I yearned for something. A change. A chance. I found both in Nicholas Fairfield. I rebelled against my parents and did what I wanted.

And what I wanted to do was Nick.

Then he was taken away from me. I was taken away from him. I went after him, went to see him right after the cops took him away but I was told he didn't want to see me. The finality of those words, the finality of the situation…nearly broke me.

My entire life ended up being taken away from me and now we have nothing. All of our assets are frozen, Dad can no longer tend to his flock—his words—Mother is weeping all the time and I can't live with them anymore. Neither can Evan. It's too stressful. Too awful.

They lost the house. Temporarily, they say, until the investigation is over. But I know the truth. Dad stole all that money and Mom knew all along. We lost the summerhouse too. We've lost…everything.

Somehow Dad had the foresight to pay for the entire year's tuition at my school so I can't get kicked out. Instead I do something worse. I go against my friends and hang with the bad girls. I move in with Evan and do whatever the hell I want because my big brother really doesn't care. He has his own issues he's dealing with.

I'm fighting against myself and I'm losing.

I'd been kept in the dark for a long time. My entire life, really. She's too young, they said. She doesn't need to know about *that*. Or *this*. Keep her innocent. Keep her pure.

More like keep her stupid.

My parents sheltered me and I knew it but I never protested. I liked living in that warm, fluffy cocoon where nothing could touch me. Hurt me. We took care of each other, Mommy and Dad and Evan and I. Dad's flock took care of us too and we took care of them. It was one big happy family.

Until it wasn't.

The cracks were there, growing with each passing day, week, month. Slowly but surely and I was oblivious.

I'm not anymore though. My eyes are wide open and I can see everything.

Every little thing.

Chapter
FIVE

Reverie, are you there?

Did they shut off your phone?

I wish you would answer me. Are you mad at me? I get it. I do. And I'm sorry.

They put me in jail. I was trying to protect you.

I miss you Daydream. I miss you so bad my entire body hurts.

I wish I could hold you. Smell your hair. Touch it. Touch you.

I love you.

Chapter
SIX

October 1st

"I'm cramping your style," I say sarcastically as I stand at the kitchen counter and wait for my bagel to pop out of the toaster. He'd picked me up last night alone, mumbling on the drive back to his place how I ruined his chances with a really hot girl he'd been trying to score with for months.

Ew. Not what I wanted to hear from my brother. I know he's a bit of a player but I don't need any of the details.

"Kind of. But I'll live." Evan ruffles my hair as he walks by, headed straight for the coffeemaker which I'd started right after I woke up, feeling bleary-eyed and worn out even after a good night's sleep.

"Like you would bring any girl around me anyway," I tease. My brother is almost two years older than me and he's good looking. I know this because I see the way girls stare at him as he walks by. There's always some girl texting him or calling him and he goes out all the time, sometimes with his friends but mostly with a girl.

But he's not the type to get serious. That's why I never meet any of the girls he sees.

As I watch Evan pour a cup of coffee wearing only sweatpants, his golden hair a disheveled mess, his eyes narrowed as he scratches his chest, all I see is my slobby big brother who's given me nothing but a bunch of grief for most of my life.

Since everything that happened with our parents though, he's really come through. We've become closer. We've had to. I feel like he's all I have and I think he feels the same.

"Just...you need to find new friends," he says cautiously as he dumps a butt load of sugar into his coffee cup and then pours in a glob of creamer before he dunks a spoon into the liquid and rapidly stirs. "Or go back to your old ones. Those sluts you're hanging out with now are doing you no favors."

"Evan. They're not sluts." The bagel pops up and I pluck it from the toaster, rubbing my fingers against each other to ease the burn from the hot bread. I start to slather on the cream cheese, irritated that he would call them names. "You're so mean."

"I just call it like I see it." He turns to face me, leaning against the edge of the counter as he takes a sip of his coffee. "They left you all alone in a neighborhood you didn't know. You went to a party where you knew no one and they abandoned you."

"And you've never done that before? Gone to a party where you knew no one?"

He makes a face. "I'm not a seventeen year old girl. Someone could've raped you, Rev."

Evan's right. I know it. But I don't like hearing it. "My friends aren't sluts," I say again as I put the lid on the cream cheese container and set the knife into the sink. Rachel might work a little fast and loose but I wouldn't call her a slut. I don't like calling girls that at all. It's a horrible word. Life is so unfair when a boy can go out and bang a bazillion chicks and no one bats an eyelash. A girl goes out and fools around with a few guys—boom, instant slut status.

"Stop rebelling." He's suddenly behind me, his big hands clutching my shoulders and giving me a little shake. "Just...be you. You're not this girl you're pretending to be. Rolling up the waistband of your uniform skirt so it rises higher and pisses off the teachers. Wearing all the makeup on your eyes and making yourself look like a raccoon on acid when you used to wear no makeup at all. Ignoring your old friends so you can hang out with ones who are out partying and giving random guys blow jobs."

My cheeks heat and I'm thankful I'm not facing Evan. Talk about embarrassing. I haven't given any guy a blow job. Not since Nick. I don't want him thinking I do that sort of thing. I might be acting the fool but I don't want my brother to think less of me.

"Go back to being you, Reverie," he says encouragingly, his speech almost working. "You know it'll please Mom and Dad."

And those particular words just ruined it. Definitely not what I wanted to hear and like I care if I make Mom and Dad happy. They certainly didn't care about Evan and me when they were doing whatever the heck they wanted. Spending other people's money and robbing everyone who believed in them.

The thing that hurts the most? They deny nothing. I've never heard Dad or Mother say they didn't do it. They just moan and cry over unjust treatment and not being able to tell their side of the story. Like anyone wants to hear it.

I know I certainly don't. Most of the time. But every once in a while, I'm curious. I'd love to hear their excuses. I'm sure that's all they have…a bunch of excuses. Meaningless words that sound pretty but have zero substance.

I shrug out of Evan's hold and grab my paper plate, taking it over to the kitchen counter and plopping onto the barstool. I eat without looking at him, without saying a word and the aggravated noise he makes doesn't startle me like I'm sure he hoped.

"I'm taking a shower," he declares as he grabs one half of my bagel and takes a huge bite out of it. I glare at him and he smiles in return. Jerk. He seems way too lighthearted this morning. I'd rather he was grumpy like me. "And then I suggest you do the same. We need to leave in an hour."

Evan exits the kitchen, his words killing what little appetite I had. I drop the bagel onto my plate and stare off into space, my thoughts consumed with what I'm going to have to face in approximately ninety minutes.

My parents.

That they let me live with Evan in the first place is some sort of miracle. That Evan wanted me living with him is even more of a miracle. Mom and Dad are holed up in some swank hotel, awaiting word on their fate. We visit them every Saturday and have lunch in their suite, listening to them drone on and on, every word positive as they talk to us like we're little innocent children who haven't a clue as to what's going on.

But we know. We're not stupid. I read the articles on the gossip sites. I watch the national news because they've even made that. A few times. Our father embezzled millions of dollars from The Flock of the

Lambs. *Millions.*

I can hardly wrap my head around it.

My phone buzzes and I grab it, checking to see who texted me.
You bailed last night.

It's Rachel.

I couldn't find you.

I typed my quick answer and take another bite of my bagel, wishing I had poured a cup of coffee for myself but too lazy to get up and do it.

How'd you get home?

Evan picked me up.

Your hot brother! Would you care if I became your SIL someday? I wanna have his babies.

Ugh. They all want my brother. It's weird.
He farts. Like all the time. And he scratches his butt. Forgets to shower. Which means he stinks.

I can deal with that.

I set my phone down, not bothering to send her another text. These girls...maybe I should listen to Evan. It's all about boys and sex and booze and skipping class. I can't remember the last time I sat down and read. I used to love to read. I pretended to love the classics but really I was gobbling every romance I could get my hands on. Historical fiction too. Oh, and true crime.

I have a serious issue with reading true crime books.

But not anymore. I don't read at all. I'm nothing like my old self.

Maybe I should reconnect with her.

Or maybe not.

"Darlings!" Mother rushes toward us as we enter the hotel suite, tragically elegant in a silk nightgown and robe, her hair perfectly styled, as is her makeup. "You're finally here. Are you hungry? Thirsty? Can I get you anything?"

Evan sends me an irritated glare before he flashes Mom a strained smile. "Sorry we're late. Traffic was bad."

It's a lie. I was bad. Resistant. I acted like a baby and told him I wasn't going with him. We got into an argument and he practically had to drag me out of his apartment. I fumed the entire drive to the hotel, refusing to talk to Evan and finally muttering an apology to him as we rode up the elevator to our parents' fancy hotel suite.

Even while in supposed exile, they do it in style. Not that I'm surprised.

"Never mind that. You're with me now." She draws Evan into her arms and smothers his face with kisses. She grabs at him almost desperately, holding him so close I swear I hear him gasp for air.

She doesn't do that with me. Evan is hers. I'm Dad's. The divide has always been there but it's even more defined now.

"Rev." I turn to find Dad standing before me wearing a suit, looking as if he's about to go speak in front of a crowd. I wonder if he misses it. Talking to people. Helping them, leading them. I wonder if he has any guilt for what he's done.

I think he did it. He's never admitted anything and neither has Mother but Evan and I have talked about it a lot. We both think they're guilty.

"Hi Dad." I let him draw me into his arms, feel his lips press against my forehead, wondering if he notices I don't call him Daddy anymore. I can't. It doesn't feel right. Innocence lost and all that crap.

Closing my eyes, I squeeze them tight so the tears that want to form don't get a chance. I want to take the comfort he offers me but it's so hard. I'm still angry at him, at Mom. But his familiar smell messes with my head and makes me forget. Makes me feel like a little girl again.

I don't like it. I want to fight against the memories and tell him to let me go but I won't. I think he needs this. Our weekly visits where we pretend for a few hours that we're a normal family.

But we're not. We never will be again.

Dad pulls away from me slightly, a frown on his face as he stares at me. "Too much makeup," he declares, his voice hard.

Immediately I roll my eyes and shrug out of his touch. "Stop." I put on the extra eyeliner, shadow and mascara just to irritate him.

"You don't need it," he says with a smile. Trying to soften his approach.

It won't work.

"You're pretty enough without it," he continues.

"Leave her alone," Mother chastises. "Let's have a nice lunch."

Lunch is anything but nice. We sit around a too-small table eating decent room service food. Mother got me a salad because I need to watch my figure and I watch with envy as Evan eats a hamburger, dunking his fries into the mound of catsup on his plate and waving them at me before he shoves them in his mouth.

He's so annoying. Almost twenty and he acts like he's ten.

During lunch, Dad talks of lies and falsehoods and Evan rolls his eyes. Mother wants to talk about memories and live in the past. Memories of when Evan and I were little and everything was sweet and peaceful and we had the lord on our side.

Those are her words. *When the lord was on our side.* I bet he's not on their side anymore, what with the way they stole from people. Innocent people, most of them elderly and the majority of them on a fixed income, who wanted nothing more than to help Reverend Hale and his flock.

If I think about it too much, all the innocent people who were affected by what my parents did, it makes me sick.

I remain silent as they talk and so does Evan. We listen to what our parents say but don't offer much in return. Not that they notice. They're too wrapped up in their problems and think they're doing the right thing by keeping us away from them. That's what Mother says every time she sees us.

I hate not having you with me Rev but I don't want our troubles to taint you. It's best you stay out of it.

Whatever. I think it's easier for them to not have us around so they can be completely selfish and worry about their own problems. Heaven forbid they want to deal with us.

"I saw something on the news about that boy who worked for us last summer," Mom says, catching my interest.

"What guy?" Evan asks, his gaze sliding to me. The look in his eyes says everything. He knows who she's talking about.

And I'm silently begging him not to say anything else.

"That boy who shadowed Michael everywhere. Nick something." Mom waves a hand, dismissing my Nick with a flick of her fingers. "He was questioned in the murder of his ex-girlfriend." She mock shivers. "Disgusting. Can't believe we had a supposed murderer working at our home."

"It's not our home," I say, my teeth clenched so tight my jaw hurts. "Not anymore."

"Well, you know what I mean." She sounds uncomfortable and her nervous laughter grates. I hate her.

I hate myself. What if I turn into a version of her someday? I don't know if I could deal.

"Leave it alone, Rev," Evan warns but I ignore him.

I'm so sick of her passing judgment on something she doesn't know or understand. He might've dumped me without a word but I know without a doubt he didn't touch Krista. He was with me on what turned into both the best and worst night of my life.

"He didn't do it."

"Didn't do what?" Mom rests a hand on her chest, her eyes wide in surprise. I bet she really did just forget who she was talking about. People mean nothing to her so this wouldn't surprise me.

"Nick. He didn't kill that girl."

"How do you know?" Mom asks, her voice sharp. Even Dad is staring at me now, waiting for my answer.

I part my lips but no words come out. I can't say it. The truth would freak them out.

I know because I spent the night with him, naked in his bed. He never left my side.

That so wouldn't go over too well.

"I just...I know."

"They talked a few times," Evan adds, sending me another one of those looks. This one says *shut the hell up before you make it worse* and I decide to take his advice.

Clamping my lips shut, I fold my hands into my lap and keep my head down. I'm done. I have nothing else to say.

I'm ready to leave.

"We gotta go," Evan the mind reader says after a few long minutes of silent, tense torture. The relieved look I send him doesn't go unnoticed.

Mother's face falls in disappointment as she looks from me to Evan. "So soon?"

"I have to be at work at five." That's not a lie. Evan found a job at a bar, cleaning tables and basically being the bartenders' errand boy. Despite how awful it sounds, he likes his job and they pay him under the table, which he loves. He told me I need a job too to help with rent but...I have no idea who'd hire me. I have zero skills. Mom and Dad can provide us no money since their accounts are locked.

"But it's only two-thirty," Dad says. He sounds as disappointed as Mother but that doesn't surprise me. They grab hold of this time together and cling to it like us being together again is going to make everything magically better.

Evan says nothing in answer. I don't either and neither do my parents.

"Next Saturday then," Mother says brightly, trying to cover up the uncomfortable silence that had just settled over the room. "Maybe you can stay longer. We'd love that you know. I understand you're busy but…"

"Sure. We might be able to," Evan says easily. Another lie. He's so smooth. His lies never trip him up. I could take a lesson from him.

He stands and starts toward the door, practically shaking Mom off as she tries to grab at him.

"Is everything okay?" Dad reaches out and places his hand over mine on the table just as I try to stand, effectively trapping me. "Living with Evan, your schoolwork…it's all going fine, right?"

I study him, see the concern etched all over his handsome face. Evan got his good looks from Dad. His attractive features are overshadowed by worry. Dark circles under his eyes, wrinkles in his face, his skin pale. He doesn't look well.

Facing jail will do that to a person I suppose.

"Everything's great," I say, pleased with how easy the lie comes. It's not so bad living with Evan, but school? That's a joke. So stupid because I need to graduate and this is my last year. I shouldn't make it so hard on myself.

But it's like I can't help it.

"Really?" he asks, his gaze dark. Intent. As if he's waiting for me to slip up and confess all. Like I'd tell him anything.

And like he cares. I've come to discover my parents are completely self-absorbed.

"Really. Everything's fine," I say firmly with a nod. I don't want to go into any more details.

I get away from Dad as fast as I can, give Mother a brief hug before I practically run out the door, Evan right behind me. I take in big gulps of air the moment I escape from their cloying suite. It's like I can't breathe when I'm with them.

It's weird how I never felt like that with them before.

"That bad?" Evan asks on the ride down in the elevator.

"Always," I say, keeping my gaze averted.

"Yeah." He pauses. "Me too."

Chapter
SEVEN

Reverie,

When it's late at night, I usually can't sleep. All I can do is think about you. Wondering where you are. Who you're with. How you're doing. I worry about you. I want you…

I have a job, working construction. It's hard work but I like everyone there and the money is good. I don't really have any friends. Michael's away at college and I miss him. The guys I work with are mostly older with girlfriends or families. I really have nothing in common with them.

You know what happened to me before and how my best friend accused me of a crime I never committed. I still don't understand why it happened. Why he said what he did. I ran into him today. David. Totally random moment in the grocery store, he was there with some girl. He told me we should get together sometime.

I don't want to. He's ruined everything. Our friendship, which meant more to me than anything else, was trashed when he confessed that we beat some guy into a bloody pulp. Why would he do something like that? He said the cops wouldn't stop. He said he finally said we did just to shut them up.

It makes no sense. He makes no sense. My life was almost ruined by his so-called confession. I know I should let it go but it's hard. My past haunts me to do this day. Krista is murdered and they automatically think I had something to do with it because of my past.

You'll never read this but it feels good to get everything out. Seeing David today...all the old resentment and anger rose up within me and I felt like I was going to burst. I had no one to talk to about it. So here I am, writing you an email you'll never get, expressing my feelings and admitting I have hatred for someone who used to mean the world to me.

I hate my ex-best friend. Sometimes I feel like I have no one to talk to and I wish...

Yeah. I have no time for wishes.

They say the truth hurts. I disagree. There's nothing better than the truth. Nothing.

And the truth is...I love you Reverie. I wish I could say those words to your face.

Again with the wishes. I'm such an idiot.

Love,
Nick

Chapter
EIGHT

October 11th

"**Y**ou're failing." Mrs. Davis looks at me from over the top of her glasses, which have slid halfway down her nose. "Two classes, Rev. History and English. Your favorite classes, I might add. This makes no sense to me considering how well you've done in the past."

She hands me a sheet of paper and I take it from her, scanning the progress report as dread fills my stomach and makes me nauseous. I have a C in Algebra 2 and I have no idea how that happened. I used to love math. The C- in Chemistry and a B in P.E. are both no surprises. I despise chemistry. I like P.E. so I can only guess the B is because I've missed a few classes.

And the two F's—I can't imagine what my parents would say if they saw that. But they won't. All mail is coming to our address at the apartment and they don't see that. If they find out I'm failing they'll make me come back and live with them, which would either be a complete joke or complete torture, take your pick.

Of course, Evan's going to kill me when he sees those grades, because he will. Better he knows than Mom and Dad though.

"I know there's been some...turmoil within your family lately," my counselor starts to say, her voice gentle, her expression kind. I've always liked Mrs. Davis. She's been helpful and sweet, guiding me well throughout the last three years. "I understand that could affect your grades tremendously. If you need any help at all I—"

"I don't need any," I interrupt her, not wanting to hear it. The sympathy, the worry, my need for guidance and all the other crap that will come with her supposed unconditional offer. "I'll do better," I say firmly, needing to believe in myself. "I promise."

She sends me a skeptical look, one that reads she doesn't believe a thing I'm saying and that's fine. She doesn't have to. I know the truth and what's inside my heart. I can do this. I *will* do this. I've always done well at school. I shouldn't mess up this last year should I? Doing bad now will only mess up my future and all because of my selfish parents don't care who they hurt and the boy who walked away from me without another word?

Not smart.

Tears prick the corners of my eyes and I blink furiously, mentally ordering them to go away. I refuse to fall apart, especially in front of Mrs. Davis.

"Are you sure? We can set you up with the tutoring program. Or you could meet with your teachers and discuss makeup assignments." She studies me, her expression carefully blank. "We'll also be calling your parents to get them involved involved though and I don't know how easily that's going—"

"No," I say vehemently. "They're not around so..." Everyone at school is aware of my parents' circumstances and that Evan is my temporary guardian until I turn eighteen. And then I'm on my own.

"But Rev. They're your parents," Mrs. Davis says. "They have to be involved."

"They're too busy with their own problems," I mutter under my breath.

Her expression turns the faintest bit harder, almost as if she's heard enough of my crap and doesn't want to deal with it anymore. That's probably a more than fair description because I've seen this same type of look on a lot of people's faces lately. People who proclaim they care yet never do anything. It's hard to help someone who's so unwilling to help herself though, right?

"We'll get your brother involved then. A progress report will be sent home in the next few days," she says briskly. "I expect to see your parents' signatures on it before you turn it in. Failure to do so will mean more trouble for you young lady, so I suggest you be truthful with them and work on picking up those grades."

"Yes ma'am." I glance down at my lap, watching as I twist my fingers together so tightly my knuckles turn white. I'd rather be anywhere other than here. Listening to her drone on telling me what a failure I am. I'm sick of it.

"You do plan on attending college, correct? Soon you'll start putting in applications if you haven't started already. You've done so well and I hate to see you mess up now and ruin everything." She's so subtle, Mrs. Davis. Telling me that I'll ruin everything.

Standing, I clutch my books to my chest, watching her as she lifts her head and contemplates me, like I'm some sort of bug she's checking out under the microscope and she's realizing she doesn't like what she sees. "May I go now?"

She lets forth an extremely frustrated sigh and nods. "Of course. See you later, Rev."

I escape her office and step out into the hallway, realizing that it's already lunchtime. I check around for a sign of a friend. Any friend. But there are none around and I'm filled with a profound loss. I miss my old friends but I blew that completely.

My stomach growls and I reluctantly head toward the cafeteria, hoping no one will pay attention to me and I can eat alone. I go through the food line, picking out a salad and an apple, grabbing a Mountain Dew to keep me awake so I can make it through the rest of my classes.

Once I pay for my food, I glance around the big room, hoping to avoid making eye contact with anyone. Not like they're paying attention to me anyway. I've always been one of the girls who blends into the walls and I liked it that way. But when I started to ignore my two best friends and hang out with other people, girls who don't really care about me, not in the way Vanessa and Valerie do, it became this thing where no one cared about me. I didn't just blend into the wall, I *became* the wall.

I start walking toward my newfound favorite corner where I sit if I'm not skipping school when I hear someone softly call my name. Looking down, I see it's Vanessa, sitting alone at what was once our favorite table. She tilts her head back, her gaze locking with mine, and I freeze where I stand.

"Hi," I say once I swallow past the lump in my throat.

She waves a hand toward the spot across from her, her expression solemn. "Sit down?"

I do as she asks without replying, setting my tray in front of me and cracking open the bottle of water I have, drinking a few swallows to moisten my super dry throat. "H-how are you?" I finally ask.

Vanessa stares at me for a moment. "Do you even care?" she asks flatly.

I'm startled. I always felt like they abandoned me but I...have to face the truth. I abandoned them. I was the one who changed, not my friends. Everything she says, how she acts toward me, I asked for all of it.

"I do," I say softly, pressing my lips together to prevent from saying anymore. "I've...had a hard time lately."

"We've missed you," Vanessa says, wincing once she made the admission. "Valerie would kill me if she knew I told you that."

Valerie was the toughest of us three and the one who hated showing emotion the most. So I know Vanessa is right. "I've missed you too," I confess. "I've been a real jerk lately."

Vanessa raises an eyebrow. "You think? Hmm, let's see. You've stopped hanging around us, ignored us when we call your name, act like the slut of the school when that's the farthest thing from the truth..."

"It's probably closer to the truth than you realize," I mumble, earning both eyebrows raised on Vanessa's part.

"I doubt that," she says, reaching out to touch my arm. I startle at her touch, shocked that she's being so nice.

"Why are you acting like this?" I ask.

"Acting like what?"

"Like you still care?"

"Because I do. We've been friends for too long for me to let a few months of you acting like a complete idiot to stop me from caring about you, Rev. Give me more credit than that."

"Well, maybe you should stop. I might not be worth it anymore," I say morosely.

"Oh my God, cut the crap." I startle at the sharpness in her tone, the way she slaps the edge of the table with her hand. "Stop feeling sorry for yourself. This 'poor pitiful me' act is getting old. So your parents screwed up, so what? Who cares?"

"I care." I jab my thumb at my chest, irritated that she would bring up my parents. "My parents didn't just screw up, they screwed people over royally, including me and my brother." I glance around before I lower my voice. "Supposedly they stole from the congregation, from the entire company. Everything we own has been seized, including their bank accounts. We could lose everything."

The sympathy on Vanessa's face is clear. She's never been one to hide anything. She's so pretty too, with her strawberry blond hair and freckled cheeks. Pale blue eyes that are staring at me like she wants to both slap and hug me all at once. "You'll still be okay. You'll make it."

"Maybe I won't," I admit, my voice small. " You don't know what's going to happen to me or my family."

"I do know one thing." She leans in close, her gaze direct, her hands clutching the edge of the cafeteria table. "You're acting like a total baby. Stop with the whining and the acting out. Skipping class and doing like crap at school, acting like a total slut when we both know you're not. You've made out with a few guys but that's it so don't tell me it's something more."

"It's something more," I whisper, my cheeks heating with embarrassment when Vanessa's eyes go wide. "I met a guy this summer and…"

"And what?" she whispers back.

"I-I'll tell you later. Just know that it got serious." I drop my head, feeling ashamed for how I've treated my friends, the two girls who've stood by me for years. I wasn't very nice to them. I don't deserve Vanessa's kindness. "I'm sorry for what I've done. I hate that I don't talk to you and Valerie anymore."

"We hate it too. We sort of hated you for a while but we're over it. At least, I'm over it. You might have to work a little harder with Valerie." I lift my head to find Vanessa smiling at me. "Do what you're supposed to do, Rev. Act like yourself. This fake Rev sucks. I miss the old Rev."

"I do too."

"Then drop the act and be normal. You'll be a lot happier I swear." Vanessa reaches across the table and grabs my arm, giving it a squeeze. "Meet up after school at the café? I'll have Valerie with me. I'll tell her to go easy on you."

Café Bella was our favorite spot to hang out at after school. We'd grab a drink and talk about our day. No one else from school would be there which was perfect. We could gossip freely. "I'd like that," I admit softly.

"Good. Then it's settled." Vanessa smiles and nods toward my tray. "Now eat your lunch and tell me which classes you're doing terrible in so we can figure out a strategy to get your grades up. Can't have you flunking out your senior year. That's just stupid."

Tears fill my eyes and I blink them away, so incredibly thankful for my friend.

I need to find my way back to myself again. I think Vanessa—and hopefully Valerie—will be the perfect guides.

Chapter
NINE

Dear Reverie,

I always feel the need to say at the start of these stupid, pointless letters that you'll never read this. I know you won't. So it'll go into my drafts folder in my inbox. I sit here typing on my phone in the dark, in my room. In my bed. The window is open, letting in a cool breeze but my skin is hot. I'm burning up with memories of you with me. In this bed. Naked and trembling and so pretty beneath me, your eyes closed, my name falling from your lips.

I miss you but I'm starting to wonder if I miss the memory of you and not the real you. Did we really know each other during our short time together? I know I certainly believed I was in love with you but I'm thinking maybe it all moved too fast. That maybe I should just hold onto our summer together as a great memory and let it go. Banish you from my mind for good.

It's hard to do that though. I want to see you again. But how? I don't know exactly where you are. I have no idea who can help me find you.

I'm going to try though. I want to know if seeing you again will

affect me as strongly as it did before. If maybe we really do belong together. Or at least if we should try and be together. That's all I want.
    A chance.

Chapter
TEN

October 11th, later that afternoon

I enter the café with trepidation, stopping when I see the back of Valerie's head, her long, silky dark brown hair pulled into a perfect French braid. She and Vanessa are sitting at our usual table, iced mochas in front of them and one in front of the chair I always sit in. Vanessa must have ordered it for me already because I know Valerie wouldn't have done so. She's going to make this difficult, I just know it but I can't blame her. I completely abandoned her.

I'm just lucky enough that Vanessa is willing to give me a second chance. Hopefully Valerie will want to as well.

Vanessa's face brightens when she spots me and she waves me over. I start toward the table, nearly tripping over my feet when I see the withering glance Valerie sends in my direction. My head starts to slowly pound with the start of a headache and I hold the back of my chair with shaky fingers, forcing myself to look at Valerie, who's watching me with a doubtful expression, her arms crossed in front of her chest.

"Do you mind if I join you?" I ask her, not sure what I'll do if she tells me to leave.

Her upper lip curls into the slightest sneer. "I suppose you can. If you want."

I deserve her anger, I tell myself as I settle in the chair, appreciating Vanessa's welcoming smile and attitude. "Thank you for the mocha," I tell her quietly.

"Thank Valerie. She paid today." She waves a hand at my angry friend as shock courses through me.

"Thank you Val," I say, my cheeks hot. I'm embarrassed. Not only because she cared enough to buy me a drink but also I don't know exactly how I can break it to them that I can't buy the drinks like I used to. I have very little money and what I do have has to go toward necessities. Definitely not expensive coffee drinks.

If Evan saw me right now he'd probably want to kill me even though I wasn't the one who paid. He's become some sort of budget Nazi, constantly telling me to take my lunch to school or yelling at me when he finds fast food bags that I threw away in the trash. He's busting his butt to pay for everything and I know I'm a burden on him.

I should get a job. But where?

"So why do you want to suddenly be with us again, hmm?" Valerie asks, getting right to the point as is her usual style. And the girl has style I can give her that. She's pretty with her pale skin and deep red hair, sparkling hazel eyes and the faint freckles that dust her cheeks and across the bridge of her nose. When I met her she always had her face stuck in a magazine, specifically fashion magazines. She loves *Vogue* and *Elle* and *Marie Claire* and swears someday she's going to work at one of them.

"Val, stop," Vanessa hisses, nudging Valerie in the ribs with her elbow. "I'm the one who harassed her first."

Val's gaze narrows as she stares at me. "Right. So *you* had to approach her. Why'd you do that anyway? She should've come to us first."

"Come on, you know why. I told you I was going to do it…" Vanessa starts but I cut her off.

"Don't blame her, Valerie. And don't fight over me either. I probably would've never got my head out of my ass quick enough to come to you two and ask for your forgiveness. I would've kept up this stupid charade forever." I clear my throat and grab my drink, taking a quick sip. They're staring at me as if I've lost my mind, which they probably think I have. I never cursed before. Not really. But I'm tired of playing games. I did have my head up my ass. "I'm sorry for what I did. I have no excuse for ditching you guys. All I can hope is that you both forgive me for being an idiot."

"I've already forgiven your idiocy," Vanessa says chirpily, laughing when Valerie and I both send her a look. "What, it's true. I'm over it. I'm just glad you're back with us, Rev. The three Vs, together again."

I smile but Valerie doesn't. I guess she's not so eager for our reunion.

"Why did you do it anyway?" When I send her a questioning look, Valerie continues. "You came back from the summer and completely ignored us. Started dressing like a tramp and hanging out with Rachel and Tally. It was weird," Valerie says with a little grimace before she takes a drink of her mocha.

"Yeah Rev. Why did you do it?" Vanessa asks, sounding a little sad, looking a little hurt. "I gotta say when you turned your back on us it hurt my feelings. Valerie's too," she adds, earning a stern look from Val.

It's hard to explain what I did or why I did it when I can hardly figure it out myself? What can I say to defend my selfish, stupid actions? So I let them talk, absorbing their questions, their angry emotions, letting the guilt and shame wash over me and take hold. But it doesn't tempt me to run away from them. I will do whatever it takes to earn their friendship back.

"We know about your parents," Valerie says, her tone unyielding. "And we really don't care. It doesn't have anything to do with you and it's not going to change how we feel about you either. You weren't the one stealing. They were."

"I still feel guilty," I admit, hanging my head so I stare at the table. It's hard to talk about my parents with anyone. Evan and I hardly talk about them and he's my brother.

"So guilty that you thought it would be better to start acting like a complete slut?" Valerie asks innocently.

"Val," Vanessa hisses but I wave her off.

"She's right. I acted like a total…slut." I grimace. I really despise that word. "I was feeling lost and confused. I went through a lot of… changes this last summer and finding out about my parents sent me into a tailspin."

"That's one way to put it," Valerie mutters, shaking her head.

"What about the boy?" Vanessa's question makes me whip my head up, panic racing through me. Yes, I promised I would tell her about Nick, but now? With Valerie's feelings still unsettled?

"What boy?" Valerie sends me a curious look.

My cheeks are so hot they feel like they're on fire. May as well get it out now. "I met a boy. He worked at my parents' summer home. His name is Nicholas." It sounds very grown up, his name. And I shouldn't call him a boy. He was closer to a man. On his own, taking care of himself, living in his own apartment and working a full-time job. He was light years above me in maturity. I behaved like a naïve fool most of my time with him.

Because I was a naïve fool. My parents sheltered me my enter life. Nothing bad ever seemed to touch me. I meet Nick and he opened my eyes to so much. Maybe even too much. Not that I regret my time with him...

"Tell us more," Vanessa prompts, her gaze rapt, expression eager.

"We spent a lot of time together," I say haltingly, not quite sure how I should phrase it.

"Did your parents know about you and this boy?" This from Valerie.

I shake my head. "They were too wrapped up in their own problems." This is far truer than I realized when it was all unfolding. Mom had been so closed off and Dad full of a forced cheerfulness that rang so false. Near the end of the summer they'd closed themselves off from Evan and me completely.

"So you snuck around?"

"Yes." I nod, memories running through my mind, one after the other. The way he looked at me, when he kissed me in the stables, when he met me in my favorite clearing for my birthday. I still have the little jar of dreams in my bedroom, hidden away in my bedside table. I take it out at night and clutch it tight, closing my eyes and thinking of him.

Stupid. So stupid.

"And it got serious," Vanessa says, though more like a statement and not a question. "You fell in love."

"We did. But then it became complicated." I take a deep breath, unsure of what I can tell them. How can I explain it when I don't quite understand what happened myself? Krista was murdered, the cops took Nick away, my parents didn't even realize what happened. Within days, the story came out. The accusations against my parents changed everything.

Everything.

Tears prick the corners of my eyes and I cover my face with my hands, willing them to stop. But they won't. They spill onto my cheeks, wetting my palms and I feel an arm go around my shoulders, tugging on me, urging me close.

"It's okay," Vanessa whispers and I fall into her arms, crying in earnest, so grateful to have my friend back, so angry to have lost the life I've always known.

So sad, so empty to lose the one boy I could've had a chance with.

"You've been crying," Evan states the moment I enter the apartment.

"Have not." My denial is halfhearted. I wouldn't believe myself I sound so unconvincing.

"Have too. You should see yourself. Your mascara's all smudged beneath your red-rimmed eyes. You look like hell." He gets up from the couch and starts to approach me.

Sniffing, I turn and head down the hall toward my bedroom, tossing over my shoulder, "Well, you can go to hell." I hate it when he talks to me like that. He's been pretty kind after everything that's happened so it's extra hurtful when he slips back into his old habits like this. And the last thing I need after the emotional afternoon I just went through.

Evan follows after me and grabs hold of my arm, turning me around so I have no choice but to face him. He looks ferocious, his eyes blazing with anger, his lips tight. "What happened?" he says through clenched teeth. "Who did this to you?"

"Wh-what do you mean?" I ask, my voice shaky, my mind scrambling. "Nobody did anything to me."

"You look like you've been balling your eyes out for hours." He slowly shakes his head, his expression just as fierce. "Don't lie to me. Tell me what happened."

"Nothing happened, I swear." I shake my head, scared and confused at his reaction. He thinks someone hurt me? "What do you care anyway?" I shrug out of his hold, baffled by how upset he seems. "Did you have a bad day or what?"

"My sister comes in looking like she's been through hell and back, you damn right I'm suddenly having a bad day. Tell me who did this to you." He grabs me again, by both arms this time, giving me a little shake.

"I met with Valerie and Vanessa after school, okay? No big deal, they forgave me for being a jerk, I got a little emotional and cried, end of story." He releases me and I step away from him, tilting my chin up, trying my best to look dignified but knowing I'm totally failing.

I swipe beneath my eyes as discreetly as I can, hoping to remove whatever lingering mascara remains. The tips of my fingers are black and I repress the sigh that wants to escape. I just really want this day to be over. "Can I go now? I want to take a shower."

"Rev." Evan runs a hand through his hair then rests his hands on his hips, frustration radiating from him in palpable waves. "It's…I heard from the lawyer today."

I frown. "What lawyer?"

"Mom and Dad's. Ours. The family's. Whatever." He waves a hand, looking irritated still. Whatever he's about to say can't be good. "He said that Mom and Dad are going to resign permanently from The Flock of the Lambs. It's done. They're done."

My jaw drops open but no words can form. It's like my tongue is leaden, my throat clogged, my lungs full. I can only wheeze out a breath, I'm so overwhelmed at what he's saying. What he's *not* saying.

"They're going to try and settle as quietly as they can. They don't want this to turn into a giant lawsuit but they have no control over that so we'll see." He clamps his mouth shut, his lips practically disappearing and I close my mouth, clear my throat. I'm already so ravaged by everything that's happened today, from learning I'm doing so badly in my classes to my confrontation with my friends, and now this?

I'm numb. I feel nothing. My reaction is…miniscule at best.

"So they're guilty."

Evan raises his brows. "You're only just now concluding this?"

"I…sure. I knew that it didn't look good, but they're not even going to fight the accusations. They're just giving in. It's like they're admitting they're guilty."

My brother says nothing. Just stares at me with this look on his face that says, well, duh.

"They did it. They stole the money." My heart breaks for the innocent people they took from, that *we* took from. I benefited from all of my parents' wrongdoing and so did Evan, especially Evan.

"Yeah. They did it." He wipes at his mouth, as if he can get rid of the disgust he feels at saying those words. "I see what you're going through and I get it. I feel like shit for what happened, Rev. I really do. The guilt is there and I know you're feeling it too. But let me say this."

At his pause I ask, "Say what?"

"We're not responsible for what they did, especially you." He points at me. "You're just a kid."

"So are you," I say softly. "This has been going on for years. We don't even know when it started."

"Yeah well, I'm the one who went on a materialistic binge. I had to have everything." So true. But when it all came up and we realized we were going to be left with nothing, he had to give up his fancy car since it was leased. Since then, he's sold the Rolex watch our parents gave him for graduating high school and I sold some jewelry they gave me throughout the last few years, even the promise ring Dad gave me.

That promise was broken the second I let Nick touch me. I forgot everything I said to my father. Every vow, every word. But most of all...

We needed the money that ring got us. This has become my life. Survival.

Chapter
ELEVEN

Survival.

That's me, trying to survive day by day. And I'm doing it damn it. The police have finally got off my back about Krista's murder. There's no evidence that incriminates me. They say my alibi is weak but they stopped questioning me about it.

Thank God. I didn't want them to go to you Reverie, but they don't even know I was with you that night. That's the way I want to keep it. I want to protect you, not draw you into this mess.

There was no solid, usable evidence left behind on Krista's body or at the crime scene. And if there was, they're not telling me anything, but that doesn't surprise me. They know she was supposed to meet me that night thanks to her dad dropping that info, trying his best to make me look like the number one suspect.

But from what I understand they're looking extra close at him. His behavior since she died is odd. They've brought him in for questioning countless times. The local news loves to talk about the murder and make him look suspect. Even though he's telling the truth about my meeting with Krista, I'm still irritated with him for ratting me out so quickly. He pointed the finger straight at me and hasn't stopped since they found her body. Anytime they talk to him he tries to drop my name but they won't let him. So he implies that her boyfriend is the one who did it.

I wasn't her boyfriend. I hadn't been for months. Yeah, we messed around but it meant nothing. She's an old friend and I hate that she died such a terrible death. You understand how I feel I hope. I can't be glad she's gone, not with the fact that she was murdered.

It sucks to admit but I don't miss her. I'm sure you don't either. She made our lives miserable.

The cops think Krista's dad is trying to divert them from him. He's their only suspect (at least publicly) and I'm not sure why. I'm not sure if I want to know why either. Krista was his daughter. I know they had a fucked up relationship but could it have been so bad that he'd end up killing her after a raging fight?

I hope not. But there's no other answer. No other suspect besides me that I know of. And I know I didn't do it.

I'm rambling. Michael would tell me I'm stuck in the past and that dude is right. I am stuck in the past. It's hard to get my head out of it when I'm constantly confronted with my past transgressions day in and day out. The cops won't let it go. They don't care that David made up the entire story about me beating that guy to death. Once in jail, always an ex-con. It fucking sucks.

I need to get over it.

Reverie, I hope you're well. I like to tell myself that I've moved on from you. Harsh, right? It's probably best that we're not together, that I don't see you, that you're not a part of my life any longer. I would only bring you down. You're a senior and you need to be having fun, enjoying your last year in high school. Doing things I never got a chance to do since I was locked up in jail (look there I go again, blah blah blah, poor me). I want that for you. I don't want you miserable.

But then I saw the article about your parents being permanently terminated from The Flock of the Lambs and I know…you must be having a hard time. I want to be there for you, holding you close and comforting you. Maybe you found someone else to comfort you though. I hate the thought of that but I have no claim on you. I'm the one who walked away and never reached out to you again.

It's all on me. I have no one to blame but myself.

So I hope you're happy. I hope you're living your life and not allowing yourself to become stuck in the past. I'm trying to do the

same.
It's hard though. So fucking hard.
Love,
Nicholas

Chapter
TWELVE

November 12th

It's been a month since I reconnected with Vanessa and Valerie. Since Evan told me that yes, our parents are thieves and liars. Since I finally wised up and stopped hanging around with people who only used me. Things have happened so fast since then I've had a hard time wrapping my head around it all.

I found a part-time job at a restaurant not too far from our apartment and it's okay. I was the hostess for all of a week but then one of the waitresses quit unexpectedly on a busy Friday night and they needed someone to cover so I stepped in. My manager, Elaine, said I was a natural and the next week I'm working as many hours as I can, bringing home an average of one hundred dollars a night just in tips, sometimes more on the weekends.

Evan's thrilled. I give him my entire paycheck and half the tips and I still have plenty of spending money. Money I usually use toward food that we need. It's sort of amazing how well Evan and I are surviving on our own. We've gone from spoiled rich kids who never had to lift a finger to hardworking, responsible almost-adults who had to grow up way too soon.

Whatever. I'm fine with it and so is Evan. Right now he's my hero and all I want to do is make him happy so he doesn't worry. I'm picking up my grades thanks to Vanessa and Valerie's help. My grades aren't at the level they were before all this stupid crap happened with my parents but they're good enough. Like I'm going to get into a great college anyway.

I can't afford the tuition.

"Keep up those grades and you can get a scholarship," Evan told me a few nights ago. "I'm not going to let your dream of getting into a good college fall apart just because of what happened."

I appreciate his opinion but college was never necessarily my dream. I just expected to make that next step naturally. Plus, Dad and Mom pushed it so hard. I needed to get into a good college. *A proper education and a bachelor's degree would help me in life.* I heard that time and again, especially the last few years.

Would going to college help me in life though? Would it really?

So I brought home a stack of financial aid applications the day after my conversation with Evan, becoming overwhelmed at the mere thought of filling all of those forms out, but I know he's right. I do have a chance and I can't let it slip by me.

I just have so little time to do anything beyond go to school, eat, work, and sleep. It's so much easier falling into bed every night, so exhausted I can't keep my eyes open for long. I prefer keeping busy, then I'm not thinking about the bad stuff.

Like what my parents did. Now they're facing all sorts of lawsuits and possible criminal charges. They haven't reached out to Evan and I since the news broke which blows my mind. It's like they forgot all about us and despite how angry we both are at them their neglect still hurts us.

And then there's Nick. Why I bother worrying about him I don't know. It's so dumb to think I had something real with him. How real could it have been since I haven't heard from him since we were separated so abruptly? That hurts too…it's like he walked away without another thought. As if I was some sort of simple summer romance and nothing more. I really didn't matter to him after all, did I?

I'm on my way to work now, my heels clicking loudly as I walk/run down the sidewalk toward the restaurant. Luckily enough I can take the city bus and the stop is only a few blocks from Seville's.

I'm also lucky because Seville's is one of the most expensive restaurants in the area. My manager Elaine knew immediately who I was when she glanced over my application and gave me one of those sympathetic looks that people are so good at lately. But other than that, she's never really referred to my family or their troubles. She's just encouraged me, pushed me and ultimately rewarded me with the quick promotion from hostess to waitress.

"It's probably not going to be busy tonight, Rev," she says the moment I walk through the door. She's at the hostess stand, going over the list of reservations for the night like she usually does. "I'm guessing it'll be an early night." She glances up at me, offering a sweet smile. I like Elaine a lot. She's got a motherly personality, always watching out for me and making sure I'm all right.

She's nothing like my mom whatsoever.

"Good. I'm glad for the break." It was a rough day at school since I worked so late last night and then went over to Vanessa's to study for a test in our government class. I didn't get home until midnight and had to wake up at six to finish an English paper. Plus with the holidays coming closer, it seems to bring more people out to dinner for some reason. I guess everyone's in a celebratory mood.

Except for Evan. And me. He already warned me he didn't want a Christmas tree this year, which I'm fine with. Why pretend to have holiday cheer when the both of us are the farthest from spirited?

The night went as expected, steady but not crazy. The customers are easygoing, with a few repeats that aren't particularly demanding. Seville's attracts a bunch of people from the neighborhood and many of them come into the restaurant at least once a week.

I like the regulars, they make me feel like I'm a part of them, how I used to feel when things were still small with The Flock of the Lambs and Dad hadn't expanded into the television show yet. The congregation felt like my family and I loved it. More than anything, I loved standing in front of the people crowding the pews as I lead them in singing hymns, wearing my pretty dresses with the matching bows in my hair.

Mom made sure I wore a new dress every Sunday once we were on TV. After awhile, it wasn't any fun anymore. Dad had to beg me to sing solos after Evan started refusing to get up on stage any longer. But I didn't want to do it without Evan. He was my lifeline when I was little, the big brother who watched out for me, who protected me. He always made sure I wasn't being forced into doing something I didn't want.

He's come back into that protective role he abandoned when he was in his early teens and I'm so thankful for him. He probably has no idea just how appreciative I am.

"Rev." One of the other waiters, Frank, sets his hand on my shoulder, startling me from my melancholy thoughts. "Can you take care of table two for me? They just need a water refill."

"Sure." I nod, ignoring my racing heart as I grab hold of a pitcher of ice water and head toward table two, which is right in front of the windows that face out toward the street. It's dark outside, even more with the ominous clouds that blew in earlier this afternoon. As I glance out the window I can see the wind blow through the trees that are lit by the street lamps, their branches swaying, the leaves long gone.

"More water?" I ask the couple at table two with a faint smile, starting to fill their glasses when they nod and say yes. I look up when the wind gusts hard against the windows, rattling them, and I see someone standing across the street. A boy. A man. His hands are in the front pockets of his jeans, his head and neck hunched into his jacket as if he's trying to fight off the horrible wind. A car drives by, the headlights cutting across his face for a brief moment and I suck in a harsh breath when I see him.

He looks just like Nicholas.

A gasp escapes me and I jerk my arm, the water and a few ice cubes spilling all over the table. The female customer shrieks and backs away, knocking me from my shock, and I set the pitcher on the table, grabbing the leftover napkins as I start to sop up the mess.

"I'm so sorry," I say again and again as I clean up the mess I made, feeling everyone's eyes on me as I try my best to clean up fast. Elaine arrives at my side, a rag in her hand and she murmurs for me to gather up the napkins and go to the kitchen.

With shaky hands and an equally shaky smile I do as she says, thankful to escape the front of the restaurant for a while. I push through the double doors and toss the soaked napkins into the trash, setting the pitcher on a nearby table. I lean against the edge of the counter, wiping my forehead with the back of my hand, and I close my eyes, irritated. Embarrassed. I've never done something like that before. I don't know what got into me.

You know what got into you. You thought you saw a ghost.

Right. That's all it was. A ghost. No way could that have been Nick. I saw him for all of about two seconds. There's no way he could've found me.

"What happened to you?" Elaine asks as soon as she enters the kitchen, her expression full of concern as she approaches me. "Are you all right?"

I nod, feeling incredibly foolish. I can't tell her what really happened. She doesn't know about Nick and even if I did tell her she'd probably think I'm crazy. "I'm so sorry. I have no idea why I spilled the water. My hands were a little shaky I guess." I hold them out in front of me, noticing that they're still trembling, and I close my fingers into fists, irritated that I'm still reacting to what—or who—I thought I saw. "I'll be fine. Maybe I should take a quick break."

"Maybe you should go on home for the night. You've been working so hard and with school too..." Elaine's voice trails off and she smiles, reaching out to pat my arm. "I think it's best if you clock out. Frank can cover your tables. It's not that busy anyway."

There went about two hours of wages and tips. I don't want to go home early. I need the money. "I can stay, Elaine. I swear. Just give me a few minutes to recuperate."

"No, I don't think so, kiddo. Time to go home. Go straight to bed when you get there, all right?" She grabs hold of both of my shoulders and looks me straight in the eye. "Get a good night's rest and come back tomorrow night ready to rock it. It's a Friday and we have a few decent sized private parties. We'll be busy."

She's not going to give in so I guess I have to instead. "Okay. Sounds good." I nod and offer a weak smile when she releases her hold on me. "I'll see you tomorrow."

I clock out and grab my coat and purse, then head outside toward the bus stop. The wind has picked up more and it blows against me, almost as if it's trying to hold me back. I struggle against it, my gaze going to the spot where I thought I saw Nick.

But no one's there.

There's really no one out tonight, which doesn't surprise me considering the awful weather. I wrap my thin coat tight around me, my head bent as I walk against the wind. It howls with a startling intensity, making me wish I had a scarf or a hat for my protection. My cheeks are ice cold and when the first drops of water fall with a splat on my face, I shake my head, withholding the groan that wants to escape. Of course, the night I wear a coat without a hood is the night that it decides to rain.

I make a run for it, ducking for cover at the bus stop, shivering as I perch on the edge of the narrow bench. Checking my phone, I see I have about ten minutes or so to wait for the bus to arrive. I tuck my phone back into my pocket before I jerk up the collar on my coat, covering my cold face as best as I can.

I'm shivering and wet, the wind blowing the rain against my back and saturating my coat. Pushing my damp hair away from my forehead, I wipe at my wet-with-rain face, grimacing at how wet my fingers really are.

Right now, I wish for the giant house we used to live in. The car Dad would be picking me up in or maybe even Evan's car, though in the past he wouldn't have bothered to pick me up. Of course, in the past I also wouldn't have had a job. I wouldn't have needed one. I had everything I ever desired, even things I didn't know I wanted.

I'm a different person from last summer. Heck, since a month ago. I've changed, even Evan has said so. But I had to. I had to grow up.

There was no choice.

A light flickers in the distance, the glow of a tiny flickering orange flame coming from a lighter, and I sit up straight, squinting into the darkness as I watch someone approach. I don't like being at the bus stop alone at night but I've gotten used to it for the most part. Someone from the restaurant usually comes with me and I like the company. Makes me feel safe.

But not tonight. Tonight I'm alone and it's freaky, especially when I know I'm not alone. I have no idea who this person is but I wait for it, bracing myself.

My heart starts to race as the flame disappears and I see the red cherry glow of a cigarette as the stranger inhales. I wait, breathless as the person approaches. I can tell he's male. Tall, with broad shoulders and an easy going stride. The horrible, fluorescent glow from the dim lights overhead shines directly on me, making it hard to see beyond the feeble light. The man comes closer, discarding the cigarette he just lit which strikes me as odd. Why waste one of those when they cost so much money? Such a filthy habit anyway but still…

And then he slowly comes into view, the light shining directly on him as he comes into the shelter, illuminating his every handsome feature. My throat goes dry as he stops just in front of me, a giant grin on his face when he kneels down so we're eye level.

"I've been looking everywhere for you," he says, his deep, familiar voice shimmering through me, making my heart trip over itself.

Making me clench my hands into fists at my sides. Fury rises within me, threatening to overwhelm, and I can barely keep it together. I can't believe after everything he did to me, those are the first words he says to me. "What took you so long?" I ask sweetly through clenched teeth.

Just before I draw back my arm and hit him square in the jaw, knocking him right on his butt.

48

Chapter
THIRTEEN

November 12th, later that night

I'm lying flat on my back on the wet sidewalk, clutching my stinging jaw as I stare up at Reverie in wonder. She looks surprised too, staring first at me, then her fist as if she can't believe she just hit me.

I can't believe she hit me either.

Pressing my hands against the ground, I brace myself and sit up, my face close to her knees encased in black pants and I briefly wonder if she'll lash out and kick me. She looks amazing, though I know she's pissed—not quite sure why—and cold and in shock. I didn't mean to scare her. Hell, I didn't mean to make her so mad.

"What in the world are you doing here?" she hisses, her eyes narrowed, her long blond hair wild from the wind and the dampness in the air. "And since when do you *smoke?*"

"I told you I've been looking for you." I stand up and settle on the bench beside her but she scoots away, taking her warmth and scent and everything that I crave about her from me. "And I only smoke occasionally." Like when I'm nervous, not that I'm going to admit that.

"It's been over three months, Nick," she says with a little grimace, my name coming from her voice the sweetest thing I've ever heard. Too bad she's looking at me as if she wants to slug me in the gut. I've never seen her so upset. "Where have you been?"

"Let me drive you home and I'll explain everything," I suggest, my fingers itching to touch her. Her hair, her face, her arm, anywhere I can grasp hold of her, I want to. I need to. Having her this close after not seeing her for so long is driving me absolutely crazy.

The bus chooses this precise moment to pull in front of the stop, the hiss of the brakes loud in the otherwise quiet of the night. The doors swing open and the driver peers through the opening, his expression full of concern. He's an old guy with bushy white eyebrows that are so low over his eyes I almost can't see them. "Hey Rev, you're early tonight."

The freaking bus driver knows who she is. Unbelievable.

"Finished work early, Ed," she says with a little wave as she stands. I stand too, confused. What is she doing? Is she actually going to get on that bus? No way. She wouldn't leave me. She couldn't.

Ed frowns as I follow her to the open doors. "This guy giving you trouble?" He flicks his chin in my direction.

She glances back at me, offering a little closed-lipped smile before she turns and—yep—jumps onto the bus. "He's no trouble, Ed. None at all." My mouth drops open as she pays her bus fare with a wave of a plastic card and she walks into the bus, settling in a seat.

The doors close, locking her inside, and I watch in disbelief as the bus pulls away from the curb and onto the street. She doesn't even look in my direction. Just stares straight ahead as if I don't even exist.

What the ever-loving fuck?

Spurring into action, I run across the street toward the parking lot where I left my truck. I can only hope that traffic isn't too bad at this hour so I can keep up with that damn bus. And I freaking hope it doesn't have too many damn stops. It's a miracle I even figured out where she works, though I haven't a clue where she lives.

I'm going to find out tonight though, I swear. She's going to listen to me. She has to. It wasn't easy for me to find her after everything that happened to her family. Both she and Evan seemed to go into hiding when the scandal broke out. She got rid of her cell phone so I sure as hell couldn't call or text her. Never had her email address and couldn't reach out to her that way. Tried sending her a message on Facebook but that didn't work either since she never replied.

So what the hell was I supposed to do? Not like I have a lot of money to make the trek to Southern California. Not sure if my truck is the most dependable mode of transportation but I finally had to say fuck it and leave. Took a few days off from work, however painful that was, and hit the freeway, headed to Los Angeles. Positive she would greet me with open arms.

That did not happen.

If she's going to reject me as outright as I'm afraid she is, then I'll be stuck getting a motel room and I sure as hell don't have the extra cash to afford that. I'll have to find the most rundown joint I can stand and stay the night there. Or crash out in my truck.

Neither option is a good one.

Hopping into my truck, I crank the engine and pull out of the lot, driving like a stupid ass in search of the bus, my balding tires screeching on the newly slick with rain roads. I tap the brake, telling myself to get my shit together and calm down. Wouldn't do me any good to get into a car accident without finding the bus, right?

And if I lose her tonight, that's fine. I can hang out around her work again tomorrow night. I'll hang out there every night until I can get her to talk to me, if that's what it takes.

She's worth it. After being without her for far too long, I realized I couldn't take it anymore. I needed to see her. I needed her.

So I went in search of her. And as if a guardian angel was smiling down upon me, I found her easily. I remembered vaguely the name of the school she went to and went there first. Watched as she hopped a city bus about an hour after school let out, cute as hell in her uniform. I followed the bus like some sort of stalker, pulling across the street when she exited the bus and walked into the restaurant named Seville's.

And she never walked back out of it. That's when it hit me. My girl was actually working for a living like me, as a waitress. Unbelievable. Today has been full of revelations. Not all of them particularly good.

The traffic light gods must be on my side because I cruise through an endless amount of green lights, coming upon the very bus I watched Reverie disappear into. I pull alongside it, staring into the dimly lit interior and I see her sitting near the window. We stop at a traffic light and I hit the brakes, sitting alongside the bus, watching her. She looks so damn pretty in her black coat, her blond hair so bright against the dark fabric, her eyebrows knit together as she chews on her lower lip, staring at nothing.

"Look at me," I whisper into the otherwise stillness of the truck cab, wishing she could hear me. "See me, Reverie. If you do, it means you still care."

She releases her lip from her teeth and presses her forehead against the window, closing her eyes. She looks like she's in so much pain, as if she's hurting and hell if my heart feels like it's fucking cracking, knowing I'm probably the one to blame. I roll down my window, blinking against the raindrops the wind blows in and I say her name, yell it into the darkness.

"Reverie!"

She opens her eyes as if she can hear me, her gaze meeting mine and I wait, my heart lodged in my throat, the lump so big I can hardly swallow.

Her lips part and she takes a breath, I see the movement of her chest as she inhales. She stares at me for a long, charge-filled moment and then she mouths one single word that splits my heart wide open.

Sorry.

Then she turns away, presenting the back of her head to me. The light turns green and the bus lurches forward but I don't move. I'm too stunned that my girl just flat out rejected me while riding the city bus.

I don't fucking get it.

A horn sounds behind me but I still don't move. I can't believe she turned away from me. Just can't freaking believe it.

I came all this way for nothing.

Another angry honk blares and I hit the gas, my tires screeching as I burn rubber across the wet asphalt. I still follow the bus, it's like I can't stop now. Anger pulses through me, settling low in my gut, fueling me, driving me on. There's no way I'm going to let her end this with a mouthed sorry and that's it. We need to talk. I need to tell her what happened. Hell, she needs to tell *me* what happened.

I track the bus, hanging back when it makes stops, keeping pace when it drives through the quiet city streets. When it stops in front of an apartment building and Reverie emerges, the relief that surges through me is almost overwhelming. Finally she's out of that trap. Maybe now I can talk to her.

I park quickly and practically fly out of the truck, following after her through the buildings, calling her name as I chase after her. It's like she hears my voice and hurries her steps, glancing over her shoulder furtively before she launches herself into a full out run.

Not deterred, I do the same, catching up with her fast, thank God. I grab hold of her arm, stopping her in her tracks and forcing her to look at me.

"What the hell are you doing?" I ask her, out of breath. Furious at her reaction, at the crappy weather, at the circumstances we're in now. I wish we could go back to the past. Return to last summer, when everything was new and tentative and exciting. When I could sneak a kiss with her in the stables and no one was the wiser beyond the horses.

"Go away, Nick," she says, her voice stern, her expression blank. She jerks out of my hold, glaring at me as she rubs her arm like I hurt her or something. "There's nothing between us anymore so just…stop."

"Stop what? Stop trying to talk to you? That's all I want, Reverie. To talk to you." I refuse to beg. There's just no way I can do that. But I won't back down without a fight either.

I'm tired of rolling over and letting shit happen to me. I need to man up and take control of my life.

"There's nothing to say. We're finished, Nick." Her eyes look like they're glistening, like she's about to cry, but then she blinks and the tears are gone. Like they were never really there and I wonder if I'm seeing things. "It was nice, what we shared this summer, but that's over. We're over."

My blood runs cold at the sound of her voice, at the finality of her words. "Is that how you really feel?" I ask, my voice so low I almost don't hear my own damn self.

She nods jerkily, her lips pressed together so tight they nearly disappear. "Yes," she whispers. "I'm a mess. You don't want to be with me. Not really."

The chill in my veins warms the slightest bit. "You're not a mess, baby. I'm the one who's a mess because I don't have you in my life."

Her expression wavers, her gaze softening, but otherwise she remains stoic. "You don't mean that. I've changed. I'm not the same person I was before when you first met me."

How could she have changed that much when it's only been a few months since we met? Though I feel like a different person since the beginning of the summer so I guess it's possible.

"I don't care. I know things have changed in your life but it doesn't matter. Things have changed for me too." I mean every word I say. I know life hasn't been fair to her lately and I want to help her. Take care of her. Make her life easier. It's hard without her, but together?

Together I think the two of us could conquer our demons and rule the world.

"Oh, Nick." She shakes her head, her eyes closing for the briefest moment as she glances up at the sky, as if she's searching for the right words to say. Searching for strength. "Too much has happened. You've hurt me. I've hurt you. I'm not the same person anymore. Not at all."

She sounds so grown up, so sure of everything, and I'm more confused than ever. How did I hurt her? All I ever wanted was to protect her. "So you don't want to give us another chance." My voice is flat, my emotions the same. I feel defeated. A feeling I'm used to. One I wanted to fight against only moments ago.

But why fight against someone who's not willing to try?

"It wouldn't be the same and you know it. I'm a different girl. One you probably wouldn't like."

I stare at her, drinking in her familiar features, her familiar smell. She doesn't look different though she's acting different, more sure of herself yet also so weary with the world. The innocent sheen is gone. Destroyed completely.

"Think about it," I say, refusing to give up. "I'll see you tomorrow, Reverie."

Before she can say a word I turn on my heel and walk away from her, not once looking back. I head straight to my truck, my footsteps determined, my mind churning with the possibilities. She may think it's over but it's not.

Not by a long shot.

Chapter
FOURTEEN

November 13th

"**D**o you work tonight?"

Nodding, I take a drink of my soda, glancing around the quad as Vanessa, Valerie and I stand outside. School let out almost an hour ago but we remained behind, working on an English project together in the library. We hit up the soda machine outside of the cafeteria and I grabbed a Coke, needing the caffeine rush before I go on to Seville's. I'm exhausted and tonight is guaranteed to be a busy one. "My shift starts at five-thirty."

"You're tied up there every Friday night. Don't you hate it?" Vanessa asks.

I snort laugh, an attractive sound I'm sure but I don't really care. I'm among friends. They won't judge. "It doesn't really matter since I have no social life beyond you two."

"You used to have one," Valerie points out, her tone the faintest shade of snide. Her smile is smug too. She still likes to poke at me for what I did to them, not that I can blame her. "For a brief, shining moment."

"A moment I'd rather forget," I say wryly, hating yet again that she brings up my minor foray into the party scene. I can't seem to escape it either. Tally approached me just the other day, asking if I wanted to hit up a new club with her on Saturday. She said she knew the bouncer and he could get us in for free, no worries on the lack of ID/underage thing.

I turned her down as nice as I could, not wanting any trouble, and Tally was cool with it. But Valerie watched the conversation go down and I think she gets a sick thrill out of beating me up about it.

"I think they'd take you back into their fold if you went to them," she says, almost as if she's daring me to try it.

"Well, I don't want to so I guess you don't have to worry about it." I roll my eyes at Vanessa who offers me a sympathetic smile in return. I swear Val is still mad at me and I don't know what I can do to change her mind. "Like I have time to party anyway. I'm too busy either at work or at school."

"What's Evan doing? Is he working as hard as you are?" Vanessa asks nonchalantly but I know there's purpose behind her question. She's had a crush on him for a while and likes to keep tabs on what he's doing, though she'd never come out and admit it.

"Harder." He feels so responsible for our wellbeing and I keep telling him I can help with as much as possible. He always blows me off though, telling me he's got it under control. I came home last night and he wasn't there, making me feel awfully alone. So alone, I'd been tempted to go after Nick last night and beg him to stay with me.

But I didn't. I can't. No matter how good he looked when I first saw him at the bus stop, how much I wanted to run into his arms and tell him to never, ever let me go, bringing him back into my life won't work right now. It's complicated enough. I don't need to add him to the mix. I can't give him what he wants. I'm not who he wants anymore.

I know it.

"What about your parents?" Valerie asks.

"What about them?" I drain the last of my Coke and toss the plastic bottle in the recycle bin as we walk by. I don't want to talk about my parents, not even to my closest friends. It's embarrassing, what's happened. How they treat us like we don't even exist. I mean really, who does that sort of thing?

Oh yeah, my mom and dad.

"Where are they? Have you heard from them? Are they sending you and Evan any money? Are they helping you at all?" Vanessa's tossing out questions with rapid fire precision and I shake my head, irritated.

"A firm no would cover all of your questions," I say grimly. I'm so uncomfortable it's not even funny. Talking about my parents is difficult, let alone admitting all their faults. "I don't really know where they are and neither does Evan."

"Wait, are you serious?" Vanessa comes to a stop, her eyes wide, expression slightly horrified. They both look surprised but they shouldn't be. This is my life now. Nonexistent parents leaving their kids on their own to figure life out, that's what we've become. While I like the independence to a point, I sometimes miss my mom and dad. More than anything, I miss the security my family represented. When we were all together, we were taken care of. That's what family does, they take care of each other. The least they could do is reach out to us.

But we don't even get that.

"Serious." I nod once and I start walking quicker, my steps determined. I want out of here. I *need* out of here. There's so much going on and it's hard for me to handle it all. And it doesn't help that Nick mysteriously shows up last night, looking so cute and sweet and so incredibly happy to see me.

What do I go and do? I ditch him. Tell him to leave me alone. Hop on the bus and try my best to get rid of him. How awful am I?

Pretty freaking awful.

That he didn't give up, that he kept coming after me, should've given me some sort of hope. But it didn't. I felt guilty, pushing him away. Why can't he make this easy and leave me completely alone? It would've been so much simpler, to stick with Evan and get through school. Once I graduate, life will become a little easier. One less thing to do.

One long life left to live, with not much hope on the horizon.

Get over your pitiful yourself.

"I'm so sorry Rev," Valerie says, her voice full of pity. She's not shown me much sympathy since we've resumed our friendship so I'm surprised. The last thing I want from my friends is pity. I don't want it from anyone.

"I don't want to talk about this." I sling my backpack over my shoulders and head toward the front entrance. I need to get on the bus soon. Get away from my friends' questions too. "I have to go to work."

"Want to get together tomorrow for lunch?" Vanessa asks.

I shake my head as I hurry toward the bus stop. "I can't. I have to work tomorrow afternoon and I have a paper to write."

"Paper on what?"

"My essay for the financial aid and scholarship forms." I am so dreading writing that paper. I have no idea what to say. And it feels like a waste of time because I'm fairly certain I won't get a scholarship or any sort of help. Not because my grades suck, but because they'll base everything on my parents' past income. It doesn't matter that all their money was taken away. They still supposedly earned it.

"Want us to help you?" Vanessa reaches out and grabs my arm, stopping me. I turn to look at her, hating the sympathy I see her gaze. "We're here for you, Rev. You know this, right?"

Smiling faintly, I reach out and pat her arm. "Yes. I know." Pausing, I fight the emotion—and tears—that threaten. "Thank you."

I have the best friends ever. Despite the fact we're making plans to get together on a Saturday night to write an essay and study for our trig test—which is just lame—they don't protest. They want to help me.

More than I can say about my own parents.

"Reverie?"

I glance up at the sound of Elaine's voice to find her standing in the doorway of the kitchen, her shoulder propping the swing door open, her expression grave. "What's up?" I ask with a feigned sort of cheerfulness that rings false to my ears.

"There's someone here to see you. He's waiting at the front."

Fear settles in my stomach and I stand, smoothing my hands down the front of my shirt. "Who is it? I need to get back on the floor since my break is up."

"You can go over your break, I won't dock you." She smiles but it's as false as my supposedly happy tone. I notice she didn't answer my question about who's waiting for me either.

With heavy footsteps I exit the kitchen and head toward the front of the restaurant, my heart racing so hard the sound is roaring in my ears. Frank sends me a sympathetic glance as I pass by him and focus my gaze on the hostess stand, where I see a tall man standing in front of the counter. He's wearing a uniform.

He's a police officer.

I flash him a polite smile as I stop beside the hostess stand, clutching my hands in front of me.

"Are you Reverie Hale?" He already knows I am, I can tell. Wariness fills me and I wish I could run but I don't.

Instead I nod, not saying a word. Good lord, it's finally happened. The cops are here to talk to me about my parents. What do I say to this man? I don't want to protect my mom and dad but I can't lie either. Not that I know much since everyone kept me in the dark.

"I'm Detective Jacoby—how are you." He reaches out, offering his hand and I take it, startled by the firm pump he gives my arm before he lets my hand drop. "I need to talk to you about Nicholas Fairfield."

Blinking, I take a step back, startled at the mention of Nick's name. That's the last thing I expected to hear. "Oh. Um, I don't know how I can help you…"

"You seen him lately?" He interrupts, his penetrating stare locked right on me and I look away, instantly uneasy. "Don't lie to protect him, little lady. I know he's come around here looking for you."

"Then why did you ask if I've seen him since you already knew?" Irritation replaces my fear. I don't like him calling me little lady. And I don't like the idea of this mom spying on me either. Standing up taller, I lift my chin and say, "He did come around but we didn't really talk."

He raises a skeptical brow. I'd estimate Detective Jacoby is around Dad's age, shorter and with a paunch around his middle. He's watching me like a hawk, looking down the slope of his large nose as if he's waiting for me to slip up. I've got nothing to hide from this man. "From what I understand you two were involved."

How in the world would he know that? Who told him? Nick? "Not any longer," I say.

"Strange that he'd come all the way here last night and you wouldn't talk to him."

"We're not together anymore. I told him that and sent him away."

"Uh huh. Bet he got real mad after all that driving when you told him to take a hike." He shoves his hands in his front pockets and leans back on his heels, contemplating me. I watch him in return, not about to back down. I don't like this man and I'm usually accepting of everyone. But after being tricked for so many years, I've come to trust no one.

I hardly trust myself, or my instincts.

"He wasn't mad." Sad and disappointed and shocked, oh yes. I can't get rid of the vision of him staring at me when I got on the bus. I know he couldn't believe I walked away from him.

I still can't believe I did either.

"You sure about that? Fairfield has a bit of a temper."

This detective is trying to bait me or scare me, I'm not sure which. "Nicholas Fairfield is the most giving, sweetest person I've ever met. If he has a temper, he's never shown it around me."

"Well, aren't you lucky then."

Sniffing, I back away from him, my butt colliding with the hostess stand. "I don't like what you're implying."

"I'm not implying anything, sweetheart. What's throwing me off is you saying you didn't talk to your boyfriend when he came to see you last night. I'm finding it hard to believe."

"I'm telling the truth." My voice rises but I can't seem to care despite my being at work. I've had it with this guy. My newfound rebellious streak decides to show itself. Authority figures don't scare me. "He tried to stop me when I left work and then again at my apartment but I refused to talk to him. I went inside and haven't seen him since. We're not together anymore. We haven't been since I came back here at the end of summer." It's the truth, no matter how hard it is to say it.

"So you live in an apartment? Where are your parents?" He changes the subject, his tone innocent enough but I see right through him.

Jerk. If he knows as much as he's letting on about Nick then he must know all about me. "I live with my older brother."

"Right. Evander Hale." He pushes his sleeve up to check his watch before he settles his gaze on me. "He's part of a murder investigation you know. Your boyfriend."

Krista. Of course, I know. "He didn't do it," I say firmly.

"How can you be so sure?"

Pausing, I press my lips together, contemplating what I should say next. The truth would be good, right? It's the least I can do. I refuse to be dishonest like Mom and Dad. Lies are destructive and the more you tell them, the bigger they grow. What my parents did, how many people they hurt, I can't change what they did. I can't take their actions back and make everything right again. It's too late.

But it's not too late for Nick. I can defend him. I can tell the truth and get the police off his back once and for all.

"I'm one hundred percent sure because the night of the murder you're talking about?" I swallow hard before I blurt out, "Nicholas Fairfield was with me."

Chapter
FIFTEEN

November 13th, later that night

Watching that jackass cop exit the restaurant where Reverie works just about does me in. Frustration threatens to overwhelm and I tell myself to get a grip but it's damn hard. I thought it was over. I thought they were letting me be because they had no evidence against me but clearly I'm wrong. That asshole followed me here and actually went in to her work to speak to Reverie. About me.

I leave her alone so I can't hurt her any longer and it works. The minute I come near her again, I bring trouble with me. If she refused to talk to me before, she'll probably try and call the cops on me now. Not that I can blame her.

I'm so pissed I want to break that freaking detective's smug face with my fist. But that would be about the stupidest thing I could ever do so I lie in wait, sitting in my truck in the parking lot across the street from the restaurant. How I missed him walking in there I have no clue but there's no telling what he might've said to Reverie.

There's no telling what Reverie might have said to him either. Not that she'd chuck me or make up lies about me because I've never been anything but honest with her. I just…I don't know what's going on and I don't like it.

The detective—I think his name is Jacoby—glances in the exact direction of where my truck is parked and I sink low in my seat, my head barely above the steering wheel I'm slumped so low. He stares hard into the darkness, looking right at me before he starts walking, headed straight in the direction of where I'm parked.

I slouch further but it's no use. He's coming for me, stops right by the driver's door and raps his knuckles on the window. "Open up, Fairfield."

Reluctantly I reach out and roll down the window, bracing myself against the brisk gust of air that blows inside my truck. "You're following me."

Jacoby doesn't bother to deny it. "We thought it was odd, that you were leaving town."

"You've been keeping tabs on me this entire time?" How'd I miss them trailing me? I got lazy I guess.

He doesn't answer. "Spoke to your girlfriend. Though she denied being your girl."

His words probe under my skin, dig at nerves. "Leave her out of this."

"Seems like she's the whole reason you came here though, right? I mean, it's not like you to took a joy ride to Los Angeles. That's pretty far to go, costs a lot of money in gas. Money you don't really have. And then she rejects you? Man, that's gotta be tough." He slowly shakes his head and makes a tsking noise.

I sit up in my seat, clenching my hands into fists. Trying to provoke me and get a reaction, see if I'll say or do something stupid. All cops are assholes. I contemplated being one and then told myself to snap the fuck out of it. "There's nothing you need to ask her so leave her alone," I mutter.

"There's plenty to ask her. Hell, if all goes as planned, she's going to be coming to the station Sunday morning so we can go over the events of the night your ex was murdered." He says the words so casually, like no big deal, but they explode like tiny bombs in my brain, giving me a headache.

"Why are you questioning her about Krista's murder?" I did my best to protect her and keep her out of the investigation. Yeah, Reverie is my alibi and I wouldn't have to deal with half this shit if I'd come out from the start and told the truth about my being with Reverie that night but I did it to protect her. She didn't need to deal with my shit. She had enough to handle already. "I've told you before she knows

62

nothing."

"She said otherwise."

Shit. Closing my eyes, I thunk the back of my head against the headrest, wishing I could take back what Jacoby just told me. "What are you talking about?"

"Your little girlfriend finally came clean with me. Don't understand why you're so upset, considering her statement is going to get you off the hook. That is, if she's telling the truth. Why you've been hiding this for so long, I have no idea, but considering you're not the brightest bulb in the light socket, there's no explaining what you do or why you do it."

I practically growl with frustration. I'm so over cops and their attitudes. "Anyone ever tell you you're a complete asshole?"

Jacoby grins, looking strangely pleased. "All the damn time."

I don't doubt that for a second.

Just past eleven-thirty I see Reverie leave the restaurant and I'm out of my truck like a damn bullet, running across the street, darting in front of a car and earning a blaring succession of angry honks for my efforts. The sound catches Reverie's attention and she stops, her expression going blank while she waits for me to approach.

I take her waiting as a good sign. I'll cling to anything at this point.

"You're here," she says, though she doesn't sound surprised, or that happy either.

I stop, keeping some distance between us so she doesn't freak out or bolt. "I need to talk to you."

She crosses her arms in front of her chest, making the black coat she's wearing bulge in a weird way. Doesn't detract from her beauty though. She's the best damn thing I've ever seen despite my irritation with her for telling the detective about our night together. "I want to talk to you too," she says.

Surprise fills me. I figured she'd want to send me packing. "Then let's get out of here." I take her arm and start to escort her across the street toward the parking lot but she drags her feet, making me stop and turn to her. "What's wrong?"

Reverie nibbles on her lower lip, the little tell that she's nervous. "Just because I'm going to talk to you, that doesn't mean I think we should get back together." Pausing, her gaze meets mine. "I don't want to give you the wrong idea."

Why is she so determined to rub that in my face? Remind me that I've blown my chance with her? I don't get it. She's not a mean person—she's the farthest from that really. I thought at one point she was in love with me. I know I'm in love with her…still. I tried to deny it but I can't. Seeing her, being with her again, even during these few stolen moments, reassures me that my feelings for her haven't changed.

But it's a false sort of reassurance I need to get over because clearly, she's over me.

"Don't worry, I get it. Whatever," I mutter as I take her hand and practically drag her across the street. It's hard to ignore the tingles I feel when I touch her but I do my best. "Let's go."

We get to the truck and I release her hand so I can open the passenger door for her. She stares at me warily, parting her lips as if she wants to say something before she changes her mind, shaking her head while she climbs inside my truck. The scent of her perfume lingers in the air, driving me crazy, and I exhale loudly, trying not to breathe it in.

Stupid.

Being close to her is going to be fucking difficult if I can't touch her. She's said more than once she doesn't want to be with me and I'll respect her wishes but damn, it's gonna be hard. Complete torture.

But to keep her safe, to keep her happy, I'll do whatever I can.

I round the front of the truck and climb inside, slamming the door and trapping her sweet scent so it completely surrounds me now. I grab the steering wheel, my grip white knuckled as I start the engine and chance a glance in her direction.

"Where do you want to go and talk?" she asks, her voice soft, her eyes luminous. My heart softens and I want to lean into her, so I can drown in her gaze. Pull her into my arms and kiss her until she can't think straight. She's thinking too much, I can almost guarantee that's what her problem is and I want to convince her that two of us—we're a good idea.

A most excellent idea, if she'd just give us a chance again.

"I don't know." She looks away, keeps her gaze fixed on her knees as she plucks at the fabric of her pants. "Where are you staying?"

I swallow past my embarrassment. I don't want sympathy but I'm not going to lie. "You're sitting in it."

She lifts her head, her jaw dropping open as she glances around the small cab of the truck. No way will I feel humiliated by my confession.

"Are you serious?"

"Where else am I going to stay? I can't afford a hotel room." I didn't plan out this trip as thoroughly as I should have. I assumed Reverie would accept me with open arms and let me stay at her place the moment she saw me.

Guess that's what I get for assuming.

"So you just came here to try and…what? Find me? Convince me we belong together? And stay in your truck like you're homeless or something?"

Her words are pissing me off. I feel like enough of an idiot, I don't need her to make me feel worse. "I'm not fucking homeless. You know I have an apartment," I mutter as I crank the engine and throw the truck into reverse, backing out of the parking spot so quick, the tires peel loudly against the asphalt.

She flinches at my words, gripping the handle above her head as she glares at me accusingly. "I didn't say you were. I just don't understand why you came all the way here without a plan. You always seem to have a plan."

"I wanted to see you, okay?" I hit the brakes at the parking lot exit and turn to find her watching me with a wild spark in her gaze, her fingers still curled around the plastic handle above her head. "I wasn't thinking. Wasn't planning. All I wanted was to see you again. You were all I could focus on. I was stupid."

Reverie doesn't say a word and we stare at each other for a long, tension-filled moment. Finally she looks away, averting her face so she's looking out the window. I pull out of the parking lot, driving aimlessly until she finally says, "We can go back to my place."

Relief fills me and she gives me directions when I ask, since I can hardly remember where I went when I followed the bus to her apartment complex last night. Other than her occasional guiding comment, she says nothing and I do the same, afraid I'm going to blurt out something stupid yet again.

I should've never admitted to her that she was the only reason I came to Los Angeles, but she had to know this right? There's nothing here for me. Only her.

"Is your brother home?" I ask as we pull into the apartment parking lot fifteen minutes later. It's starting to sprinkle, the rain dotting my windshield and blurring my ability to see but I still haven't turned on the windshield wipers. I don't want to face Evan. He would probably try and kick me out, not that I can blame him. I'm the asshole that took his sister's virginity and made her cry.

"No, Evan's at work. He won't come home for hours." She smiles ruefully. "We both work a lot now."

"Complete turnaround from a few months ago, huh?" I park my truck and turn off the engine, pulling the keys out of the ignition. I clutch them in my hand, the metal digging into my palm as I turn to face her.

Her smile turns real and seeing it sucks the breath out of my lungs. "Yeah. It's kind of crazy, how much my life has changed."

"Trust me, I get it. One minute everything is good and then the next, it can all change. In a blink of an eye, all because of what someone else did, not because of your own actions."

She contemplates me, tilting her head, her long, wavy blond hair spilling over her shoulder. "You do get it, huh. After everything that happened to you, when your friend betrayed you, were you scared?"

"Yeah. I was." More like I'm scared she's gonna reject me for good and send me away. And I don't want to get out of this truck. I like the way she's talking to me, looking at me. Like she trusts me again. "Your parents betrayed you too."

"They did," she agrees, nodding once. "I feel…guilty."

"You didn't do it," I point out, surprised she'd say such a thing. "You didn't steal all that money."

"But I spent it. I benefited from what my parents did. I lived an amazing life that was funded dishonestly. I wish I could pay all of those people back."

"That's not your fault. You're just a kid, Reverie." Giving in to my urges, I reach out and touch her, let my fingertips graze the ends of her silky soft hair. She doesn't flinch, doesn't pull away and I take advantage by touching her again. "You can't blame yourself for your parents' mistakes."

She leans into my touch and I cup the side of her head, threading my fingers fully into her hair. Her eyes close and I swear she's going to cry. "But I do. I can't help it. Don't you ever blame yourself for your friend's mistake, when he said you killed that guy? Did you ever feel responsible?"

"No." I never did. What David did to me was unforgivable. I don't think I can ever accept his apology. He almost ruined my life. "But I do feel guilt over what happened to Krista."

Reverie stiffens and pulls away from my touch, moving away from me so far that the distance between us suddenly seems endless. The air goes frosty as her expression goes completely blank and she reaches for the door handle. "Let's go."

I follow her up to the apartment she shares with her brother, mulling her lack of comment regarding my guilt over Krista's death. Krista was a complete pain in my ass and tried her best to ruin our relationship any way she could. I can't help but feel bad for what happened to her though. I'd known her since we were little kids. We'd been friends for years. Yeah, the bad stuff at the end sucked but no one deserves to die like Krista did. I want to help find her killer but it's kind of hard when the cops focus so much on me.

Assholes.

We enter the apartment and Reverie flicks on the lamp near the front door, illuminating the room with soft golden light. There's not much furniture and what's there is simple. I watch as she moves about the room, setting her purse and backpack on the dining room table before she goes into the kitchen.

"Want something to drink?" she asks.

"Water is fine. Thank you." I sit on the edge of the couch, bouncing my leg nervously as I wait for her return. I'm not going to put her out. I'm not going to stay long either because clearly this isn't going to work. She doesn't want to have anything to do with me and I'm not going to push it.

All I want to talk about with her is why she told the cop we were together the night of Krista's murder and that was it. I'll hop in my truck, buy a giant coffee or soda at a convenience store and get the hell out of here. Go back home where I belong. In Nowheresville doing nothing.

She brings me a cold water bottle from the refrigerator and I thank her, twisting off the cap so I can take a swig. Reverie settles in the overstuffed chair across from the couch, her expression expectant, her hands gripping her knees as if she needs to brace herself against whatever is about to be said.

"You shouldn't have talked to the detective," I finally say, earning an eye roll from her.

"What am I going to say? Leave me alone? Tell him to go?"

"Yeah, absolutely." I set the bottle of water on the tiny table to my left. "You don't owe him anything. Tell him to call your lawyer or whatever."

"I don't have a lawyer," she admits softly.

Well, that's shocking. I'd figured the entire Hale family needed a lawyer after everything that had happened. "I wish you wouldn't have said what you did to him."

"All I did was tell him the truth." She shrugs. "Why didn't you tell the police you were with me from the beginning?"

"Because I didn't want you to be involved."

"I was already involved, from the very beginning I've been a part of this but you pushed me away. You never came back for me, Nick. I had no idea what happened."

"They stuck me in jail, that's what happened." I stand and start pacing, fighting off the guilt, the pain, the irritation...all the emotions that are flooding me at once. "They held me for questioning for forty-eight hours. Tried to break me down pretty much the entire span of those forty-eight hours too. By the time they let me out and I went back to your house, you were gone."

I remember the feeling of rushing to get to her the minute the police released me, my heart racing the entire drive to Hale House. When I got there, the house was dark and quiet, the grounds seemingly abandoned and I knew before I even attempted to knock on the door they were gone.

For good.

"We came back here early. I told you that was going to happen," she murmurs. "My parents wanted to get us back so they could...take care of legal matters."

Huh. Yeah, that went real well for them. "You shouldn't have told that detective about us being together that night, Reverie. I didn't want to get you involved in this mess. I was trying to protect you."

"By hurting yourself in the process? That's the dumbest thing ever Nick, and you know it." She stands, her cheeks red, hands resting on her hips. "I'm your alibi, proof that you couldn't have been the one who killed Krista that night yet, you kept your mouth shut."

"I know, but I didn't want you involved in this." I stand too, towering over her, hating how she cowers away from me ever so slightly. "I knew your parents would flip out if they knew we spent the night together and that's how you became my alibi. I didn't want to get you in trouble."

"They weren't even paying attention to me. They were too wrapped up in their own problems." She'd shed her coat when she first entered the apartment and she looks damn good in the simple white button-up shirt and black pants. There's a stain on the shirt though, low on her belly, and the fabric is wrinkled. She's nothing like the girl I left behind, nothing at all. "I missed you," she admits.

My heart cracks. "I missed you too, baby. I was climbing the walls trying to find you."

"I'm sorry. Maybe...maybe it was for the best." She wraps her arms around herself and holds on, looking small and sad. "Things are so different now, Nick. And so am I. You probably wouldn't like me anymore."

I take a step toward her, ready to convince her otherwise. "There's no way that could be true."

"I hardly recognize myself. When school first started I went sort of...wild. Going out to parties, meeting boys."

My muscles tense and I try not to show any outward reaction. "What sort of guys?"

"Jerks who were only looking for one thing. Sometimes I let them...touch me."

Closing my eyes briefly, I will myself to stay under control. I had no claim on her then, though she's always been mine. "I don't know if I want to hear this."

"It didn't last that long. I got over my rebellious streak quick." She laughs but there's no humor in the sound. "I never heard from you again, you refused to see me when I went to the jail looking for you. My parents were neglecting us...it felt like no one cared about me. So I decided I didn't care about me either."

"Reverie..." I start toward her but she holds out her hand, stopping me.

"Don't." She shakes her head, her expression forlorn. "I don't want your sympathy. I snapped out of it quick. I have my brother. I have my friends. I don't need anyone else."

Including me? I want to ask but I don't. She's hurting. She thinks I abandoned her. I need to convince her I didn't. Not really.

Yeah, fine I turned her away when she came to the damn jail the day after they kept me for questioning about Krista's death. The fucking cops encouraged me to go talk to her, probably hoping I'd slip up, but I refused. I wasn't going to put her through that.

I didn't want her to see me like that either.

Protecting her only ended up fucking over my chance with her. I think I may have ruined it.

For good.

Chapter
SIXTEEN

Early November 14th

Evan came home from work earlier than expected, much to my relief. Nick and I had settled back in our respective seats after our discussion got a little heated. Then our conversation turned into me trying my best to dodge his questions about my parents. Despite how close we were, I'm not comfortable talking about what Mom and Dad did with him. I'm not comfortable talking about it with anyone, only Evan. And that's because he's the only one who understands how I feel.

Spending time with Nick alone, I can feel my defenses wearing down, minute by minute. Just looking at him is a temptation I find hard to resist. I want to go to him so bad and curl up in his lap, feel his strong arms wrap around me and hold me close. He looks so cute in his jeans and light gray hooded sweatshirt, his hair a little wild from the moisture in the air outside, the golden highlights from the summer sun I loved so much now gone. They must've been trimmed off and I silently mourn the loss.

So silly.

"What the hell is he doing here?" Evan asks the minute he walks through the door and spots Nick sitting on the couch. "You brought back the help? Did you tell him we can't pay as much as Mom and Dad did?" He laughs at his own joke but I ignore him, focusing instead on Nick's expression, how irritated he looks, but he restrains himself from saying something awful in return.

I'm thankful. The last thing I want is for him and my brother to go at it.

"Seriously, Rev." Evan stops by the chair I'm sitting in, peering down at me with that protective older brother vibe radiating from his tense body. "What the hell is he doing here?"

"I'll leave." Nick leaps to his feet, obviously uncomfortable, and I stand as well, going to him.

"No." I rest my hand on his shoulder and he glances down at where my fingers rest before he lifts his head to meet my gaze. "Stay here with us tonight."

"Oh, hell no," Evan starts but I turn to glare at him, shutting him up.

"I couldn't..." Nick's voice fades when I send him the same look.

"He has nowhere else to stay. I'm not going to let him sleep in his truck again and neither are you, Evan." I pause, letting that information sink in. "He's going back home tomorrow, right Nick?"

"Yeah." He pauses and shoves his hands into his front pockets. "Though don't you have to go back there with me?"

Crap. Why did he have to bring that up now? I did promise Detective Jacoby I would return to the town where I spent so many summers so I could make an official statement in regards to my being with Nick during the night Krista was murdered. But I hadn't planned on telling Evan about this.

How else were you going to get there? Take a bus? Hitchhike?

My logic isn't always the best. I never think things through enough. I remember Mom and Dad both telling me this but I always blew them off. Guess they were right.

"You're not going back there with him. No freaking way," Evan says, sounding outraged. I should be mad at him trying to stop me because hello, he's not my dad, but all I can do is appreciate his concern because no one else seems to have it for me. At least Evan wants me safe, and I love that.

I shoot an irritated glance in Nick's direction before I start explaining. And by explaining, I tell Evan everything, even the hard stuff—like my staying the night at Nick's apartment when Krista was murdered—but I don't give him all the dirty details. I can hardly get the words out that I spent the night at Nick's place without blushing.

Evan can figure out on his own without me saying what exactly I was doing with Nick.

I still can hardly believe I actually had sex with Nick. It's been so long, I can almost imagine the entire summer was a dream. That I didn't get naked with him, didn't touch him everywhere, feel his soft, warm mouth slide all over my skin before he slid inside my body…

Shaking myself, I focus on my brother. "So I have to go," I say. "I have to give my statement and help Nick. They'll leave him alone when they know he has a solid alibi."

"Well, I can't take you. I have to work all weekend. And don't you work tomorrow?"

I nod. "Only in the afternoon, during the lunch rush. We can leave after I get off work. Is that okay, Nick?"

He nods, his face somber. "That's fine."

"Yeah, I bet it's fine. Then this means my sister will have to stay the night with you. Not under my watch dude," Evan sneers. "Just because our parents weren't paying attention doesn't mean I'm not."

"Evan, stop," I say softly but he's not listening.

"Besides, she has school. She can't leave. So you can forget about your alibi over a freaking *murder*. Who the hell are you anyway? What sort of kid finds himself involved in that sort of heavy shit?" Evan steps closer to Nick, until he's practically in his face. I step away but Nick doesn't back down and fear claws at my throat. If they start fighting…

"Did he put you up to this, Rev? Are you lying about being with him that night?" Evan asks, never taking his eyes off of Nick.

"Hell no, she's not lying. I tried to protect her. I never mentioned her name to the cops once," Nick says. "I couldn't risk it."

"Risk what? Getting caught?" Evan asks skeptically.

"Ruining her reputation."

My heart melts. Just turns into a puddle of goo in the center of my chest. That he cares so much about me and my reputation when I was acting the fool the moment I got away from him, makes me want to both hug him for his thoughtfulness and smack him for putting his future on the line.

Evan slides me a look as he mutters, "This guy is unbelievable." But he steps away from Nick, much to my relief, and I go to him, resting my hands on my big brother's shoulders so I can give him a little shake.

"Thank you," I whisper, standing on tiptoe so I can press a kiss to his cheek. His shoulders sag beneath my grip and I stare at his face, see the exhaustion around his eyes, the downturn of his mouth. My brother is worn out. It's a look he's been wearing for weeks. Months even. "Go to bed. I'll be fine."

"He lays a hand on you and I'll murder him." Evan says it loud enough that Nick can hear and I'm sure he did that on purpose. Big brother is anything but subtle when he's in this mode. "He sleeps on the couch, Rev. Nowhere near you, you got it?"

"I wouldn't sleep anywhere else," Nick pipes up.

Evan turns on him. "If I said you're sleeping on the cold ass vinyl floor in the kitchen, then that's where you'd sleep too. This is *my* house. Never forget it."

Before Nick can utter a word, Evan is gone, locked away in his bedroom, the door shutting with a loud slam.

"I meant that I wouldn't expect to sleep in your room or in your bed, Reverie," Nick explains. "I get where I stand with you and your brother, and I would never try to cross that line."

"I know." I suddenly feel so weary, I'm afraid I'll drop right where I stand. Work was busy and talking with Nick, dealing with Evan...I'm exhausted. "He's just being the protective big brother."

"He does a good job at it then," Nick mutters with a slight smile and I can't help but smile in return. It's—nice, spending time with Nick. I've missed him. I already knew this and tried my best to deny it. Eventually, with everything else going on, I started to forget how being with Nick made me feel.

And no one makes me feel the way Nicholas Fairfield does with just a look. A smile. A touch. A kiss...

I'm fighting against those other, more complicated feelings. The ones that surge up when he smiles at me like that. I remember the taste of his lips, the way they felt against mine and I think...

I still want him. I still lo—

"I have a blanket in my truck I could bring up," he says, interrupting my wayward thoughts. "If you don't have any to spare."

"We have a few. Let me grab them." I go to the hall closet and pull out a couple of throw blankets, then dart into my room to grab a pillow from my bed, before I bring it all to him.

"Thanks," he says as he takes the throws and pillow from me and sets them on the couch.

I stand there, unsure of what to do, what to say next. "Um, did you bring stuff with you?" I ask. "Maybe a bag with a change of clothes or something?" My cheeks are hot again which is so stupid but all I can think about is his underwear and that is about the dumbest thing ever.

What am I, twelve?

He always looked real good in just his underwear. He has a nice chest. Broad shoulders. And a great...

"Yeah, I'll go down and grab it right now." He goes to the front door and opens it, the whisk of wind blowing through and bringing with it a scattering of raindrops. He reaches behind him and yanks up his hood, obscuring his head. "I'll be right back."

The door shuts and I'm off to my room, changing out of my smelly work clothes as fast as I can, throwing on a pair of plaid fleece pajama pants and an old white Henley top I've been sleeping in for years. I go to the mirror above my dresser and try to smooth out my messy hair, my gaze dropping to my chest. My boobs look huge in the tight top and I reach for the hem, ready to change out of it since I'm sure Nick will think I'm trying to tempt him or something, when I hear him knocking on the front door.

Crap.

Giving up on changing the top, I rush to the door and let him in, chastising him that he doesn't need to knock since I didn't lock the door behind him. Which leads him to give me a speech about how I should always keep the door locked because who knows what sort of creepers are out there lurking?

Yikes. Men. They're always on my case lately.

His sweatshirt is speckled with rain and when he brushes the hood off his head, he flicks drops in my direction, making me wipe at my face with a giggle. He smiles at me and drops his duffel bag on the ground, reaching up with both hands to run his fingers through his already messed up hair until he's gripping the back of his head. The faint smile stretching his glorious mouth is strained and there's an unfamiliar light in his eyes. He looks about as uncomfortable as I feel.

"This is weird," he declares.

I can't help but agree. And appreciate his honesty. "It is. But we can make it work, right? It's just for tonight. I can't let you sleep in your truck again, Nick. It's too cold outside. I'd never forgive myself if something happened to you."

"Yeah, it is pretty damn cold out there. Thanks for letting me stay." He shoves his hands in his pockets and hunches up his shoulders. He looks nervous. I'm nervous too. "You sure Evan doesn't mind me being here?"

"He probably hates that you're staying the night, but he'll get over it." I take a step toward him and pat him on the shoulder, marveling at the solid feel of muscle beneath my palm, beneath the thick fabric of his sweatshirt. Has he gotten taller since the last time I saw him? Broader? He's so big, standing next to him makes me feel small. "Do you need anything else?" I remove my hand from his shoulder, wishing I could touch him more.

"Nah. I'm gonna change, brush my teeth and go to sleep." He smiles, looking cute, like a little boy, and my heart flutters. When he reaches for the hem of his sweatshirt I step away, watch in silent fascination as he pulls the fabric over his head, taking the T-shirt he's wearing beneath it upward so I catch a glimpse of his flat, perfect stomach, the little trail of dark hair that starts just under his navel.

I'm breathless, my skin is tingling and when he tosses the sweatshirt onto the couch, I start to walk backwards. "Okay well, goodnight." I need to get away from him before I do something really stupid.

Like jump him.

"Night, Reverie," he calls after me as I hurry to my bedroom. Glancing over my shoulder, I find him watching me with that penetrating, thoughtful gaze and I turn away, practically tripping over my feet in the hall. I rush into my room, shutting the door quietly before I slump against it, closing my eyes and pressing my forehead against the rough wood.

My feelings for him haven't stopped. I still want him. I'm still in love with him. So why am I denying myself from being with him? Because I've changed and I'm worried he won't accept me for who I really am? And because my life is so crazy the last thing I need is another complication to muck it all up?

Valid reasons, but why would I deprive myself from being with him? He's the only one who understood me. Who listened to me. Who cared about me.

I think he still does.

Cracking open my eyes, I push away from the doorway and shut off the light before I crawl into bed. I lay there in the dark, listening to him move about inside the bathroom, which is right next to my bedroom. He finishes brushing his teeth before he exits the room and I swear I can feel him standing on the other side of my closed door, waiting. Listening for any sign of life coming from within.

I can't move. I'm frozen, holding my breath, waiting for him to knock on the door, to turn the knob, anything to show that he wants to see me. I want him to both respect my brother's wishes and defy them. I want him overcome with need yet cautious. I want…everything.

All of him.

Disappointment crashes through me when I realize he is definitely obeying Evan's wishes. He doesn't sneak into my room, doesn't attempt to talk to me, nothing. I should be happy. Pleased that he doesn't want to upset anyone.

Instead, I'm sad.

Rolling over on my side, I punch the pillow beneath my head and settle in for the night, willing myself to fall asleep. I get to spend pretty much the entire weekend with him. Maybe we can work it out then since we'll have plenty of time. But for now I'll have to settle for Nick visiting me...

Only in my dreams.

Chapter
SEVENTEEN

The longest night/morning ever…

I can't fucking sleep, not while knowing Reverie is just steps away from me, tucked into her bed, all cozy and cute in that tight white top that shows off her curves and the fuzzy pajama pants. I want to sneak into her room and crawl into bed with her. Hold her close and press my face against her neck, kissing the soft skin just behind her ear. Teasing little kisses that'll wake her up nice and slow until she's turning into my arms and wanting more.

Just like that, my body reacts and I growl in frustration, staring up at the ceiling. The couch is narrow and short and my feet hang over the end, which sucks. Light from the various electronics that are scattered throughout the living room and kitchen cast the place in a dim glow and I can hear the occasional car passing by outside, the sound of rain falling, the rhythmic gust of wind rattling against the building.

It's cold as hell too, the thin blankets not offering much protection against the chill air, but I hate wearing too many clothes when I sleep so it's my own damn fault I'm cold. The Hales aren't using central heat and I'm guessing that's because it costs too damn much. Such a switch from their privileged life I witnessed all last summer. Evander Hale lived like a damn king with his designer clothes, expensive Rolex watch and crazy ass car that no teenager should be allowed to drive. Now he's working his ass off, barely making it and trying to take care of his sister.

Wild.

Seeing Reverie in her new element only makes me respect her more. She's so strong, so smart, so determined to do what she can to survive. I admire her guts. In the past I had zero guts because I naively believed the system would take care of me after David accused me of being a murderer. Considering how well that worked out for me, I finally learn how to stand up for myself, only to have the system come after me yet again.

Well, screw that noise. I'm over it. Starting now, my life is going to change. It has to. I need to get the police off my back once and for all. First step, Reverie's statement that she was with me the night Krista died. Reverie's right—why would I protect her only to put my own future at risk? Crazy.

Second step? Somehow convincing Reverie that we belong together. That might be harder to accomplish but I'm determined to make it happen.

Closing my eyes, I breathe deep and tell my ass to go to sleep. It's already close to two in the morning and I have no idea what the plan is when the sun comes up. Reverie said she has to work in the afternoon and I know Evan is working too. Where does that leave me? Is she definitely going with me like we discussed? Or is Evan going to take over and handle everything?

I don't want Evan coming between us. If I can get her alone, get her to come back with me I can make this happen. I can make *us* happen.

I hear a noise in the hall and I crack open my eyes to see a golden strip of light shining beneath the closed door of the bathroom. I have no idea if it's Evan or Reverie behind that door but I do know I have my preference. And when the door opens no less than a minute later, a gorgeous leggy blonde stepping out into the hall, I sit up, softly calling out her name. For a moment, I almost fear she didn't hear me, but then she turns in my direction, a little smile curling her perfect lips. The relief that floods me as I watch her approach is near overwhelming.

I have it so bad for this girl and she doesn't have a clue.

She walks toward me, her hair mussed, her expression sleepy. "Did you say my name?" she asks.

"Yeah."

Her eyebrows scrunch up in that way they do when she's confused. Damn, she's cute. "You okay?" she whispers.

I sit up more and scoot over, patting the space beside me. "Come here." I gather the blankets into my lap because I'm only wearing my boxer briefs and I don't want to scare her. She's seen me in less but I don't want to mess around like that with her brother in the next room. Besides, she's not ready for that. I'm not going to push too hard. The last thing I want is to send her screaming, running away from me and shutting down my chances with her.

"Reverie?" She doesn't move, no sound, no answer comes from her and my heart feels like it stops beating for an infinitely long second before she settles on the couch by my side, her warmth seeping into me, she's so close.

"I shouldn't do this," she says into the darkness, facing away from me. "I should go back to my room."

I touch her hair, flip it over her shoulder so it flows down her back. "Don't go." It's all I say, a simple request that I hope like hell she meets. "Can you sleep, knowing I'm out here?"

"No," she admits, her voice sounding choked. "But that doesn't mean anything, right? It's not like we're together anymore. Everything's so different now, including you. Including me."

"And that's a bad thing? If you think you changing bothers me, you're wrong." I skim my fingers across the length of her shoulder, down along her upper arm, feeling her shiver beneath my touch. I wish I was touching bare skin. "I like who you've become."

"You don't know me. Not really," she counters.

"I want to. And I think we got pretty close over the summer, don't you?"

She looks at me then, her eyes wide in the darkness, her lips parted. "I was such a different person then and you know it. I had...no clue."

"I know." Leaning forward, I pull her into me, wrapping my arm around her shoulders, my mouth at her ear. My skin feels electric coming into contact with her, even though she's almost completely covered. I close my eyes, battling against all the urges I have to throw her down on the couch beneath me and strip her naked. "I taught you a lot."

She smiles, tilting her head away from mine. "Stop."

"Stop what?" I press my lips to her cheek, offering her a lingering kiss that I want to take further. Further and further until we're too far gone to care.

"You're teasing me." The smile fades. "Making fun of the inexperienced girl."

"No way." I let my lips drift across her cheek, toward her ear, until I'm nibbling on the lobe and making her squirm. "I love that you were so inexperienced. It means that you're all mine." Being with her, having her in my arms, the possessive urge that sweeps over me is hard to deny.

This girl is definitely mine, though I'm not sure she realizes it.

A shuddering sigh escapes her and she hangs her head down. "I've been with other boys."

I stiffen and pull away from her, curling my fingers around her chin and forcing her to look at me. "Hell, Reverie. Did you…have sex with them?" Anger bubbles up inside me and I tell it to fuck off. I have no right to be mad. We weren't together. She was feeling lost, missing her old life. I can't blame her.

But I want to tear apart every one of those guys who had their hands on her, no matter how brief the interlude was.

She slowly shakes her head, her eyes glittering with unshed tears. "I kissed them, that's it, I swear. I think…oh my God, this is going to sound so stupid but I think I was trying to kiss you out of my system or something."

"Did that plan work out for you?" I ask, my voice low, my thoughts turbulent. I'm quietly freaking out inside waiting for her answer and I don't know how long I can stand it.

"No." She loops an arm around my neck, pulling herself into me. "I still missed you."

Gripping her by the waist, I haul her into my lap, until she's straddling me, her knees on either side of my hips, slender hands gripping my shoulders, her fingers pressing into my skin, making it sizzle. "You miss me now?"

Reverie nods, her voice soft, her eyes heavy as she stares at my mouth. "Yes."

It's the aching whisper of her voice that urges me into action. I kiss her, my mouth settling on hers, our lips connecting, our bodies pressed close together. My body instantly reacts to her taste, to the way she touches me, her knees pressed hard against my hips, the eager little noises that escape from the back of her throat when I part her lips with my tongue. I haven't kissed her in months and the rush that comes when I touch my tongue to hers for the first time since forever spurs me on.

I'm going to have to exercise some serious control tonight or she's going to be naked in seconds. That's all I really want. I think that's all she wants too but I'm not about to risk her brother discovering us like this. He'll hand me my ass on a platter for screwing his sister on his couch.

And I'd like to keep my ass, thank you very much.

"Nick." She whispers my name after breaking our kiss, bending her head so she can kiss a path of heat along my jaw. My arms tighten around her waist and I want to shout in triumph that I have her like this. "I need to go back to bed."

Say…what? Pulling away from her slightly, I give her a little shake so she lifts her head, her gaze meeting mine. "What did you say?"

"I keep kissing you like this and I'll want more." She skims her fingernails down my chest, across my pecs and yeah, I'm instantly, painfully hard. "And I don't want to move too fast."

Says the girl who came to my apartment and jumped my bones a few months ago. But she's right. I know she's right. We need to get through all of this, one step at a time. We shouldn't cloud our judgment with a night of awesome sex.

Though that sounds pretty damn good right now.

"You're right." I lift her up and set her away so she's sitting on the couch next to me once more, the both of us breathing a little too hard. My heart is racing and I feel like I'm on edge but damn it, I'm going to respect her wishes. "Go back to your room."

She gapes at me. "Nick. Really?"

I need her to stop contradicting herself. She wants me. She doesn't want me. I understand her struggle, as much as it frustrates me. "Yes." I nod and stand, grabbing her hand so she has no choice but to stand with me. "Go to bed, Reverie. We'll talk in the morning."

Her face falls and I pull her to me, kissing her for a long, deep, wet minute so when I break the kiss, she wobbles on her feet, her dazed expression filling me with satisfaction. "Night," I murmur against her lips before I give her one more lingering kiss.

She heads for her bedroom with a weird little smile on her face, closing herself away within seconds. I collapse on the couch, my mind a disastrous mess because that was the most intense ten minutes of my life and now she's gone.

Fucking head trip is what that girl is giving me, not that I'm pushing her away. Hell, I'm reveling in the head trip, as fucked up as that sounds. The push and pull, the back and forth, it's all worth it if the ultimate reward is Reverie in my arms.

Forever.

Another door opens and this time it's Evan in the hall, wearing a pair of sweats and nothing else. I brace myself, knowing he can see me, that he can tell I'm awake and yep, here he comes, a grim look of determination on his face as he settles into the chair across from me.

"You're awake," he says.

"So are you." Obviously.

"And Rev just went back into her room," he states as fact.

A fact I can't deny. But I won't confirm either so I say nothing.

"You're lucky I didn't find her out here with you. I won't hesitate to kick your ass."

"We were just talking." With our lips and tongues and no words being said but yeah. Let's go ahead and call that talking.

"My ass, you were just talking. But whatever, if that explanation makes you happy then we'll go with it." Evan leans forward, clasping his hands in front of him as he peers up at me. "Let's get a few facts straight about my sister."

Great. At the rate I'm going I won't get any sleep tonight. "All right," I say cautiously.

"She got all fucked up after what our parents did to us. Fucked up over what you did to her too," he says, silencing me with a look when I'm about to open my mouth to protest. What the hell did I do to her? All I ever did was love that girl.

"But she's strong, my sister. I'm proud of Rev. She works hard, she's doing well at school again and her friends are helping her out. Her life is on track the way it should be. I have a feeling she'll get into a great college and then everything I've ever done for her won't be in vain, you know?" He sounds like her dad, not her big brother. But it's kind of…nice, for lack of better term, to see the perpetually spoiled rotten Evander Hale step up and take care of his sister. I'm impressed.

"What about you?" I ask. Didn't he have plans? He's given everything up, sacrificing it all for Reverie, but what does Evan want?

"Me? I'm fine. Doing what I do." He blows off my words and I let it be. "It's you I'm concerned about."

"I'm not going to do anything to ruin Reverie's chances to get whatever she wants. I'm here to encourage her not hold her down," I say.

"You know what I see when I look at you?" At my shrug he continues. "Someone who'll definitely hold her down. Hold her back. And that's the last thing I want. So if that's your plan, then you better keep on going. She doesn't need you to come back into her life and fuck it up even worse."

"That is the last fucking thing I want," I say vehemently. "You can trust me."

"Ha, right. Listen asshole, I trust no one. Not after what happened. Rev doesn't trust anyone either. Just…don't hold her back. Let her do her thing. Go back home and let her finish school. That's the most important thing for her to do right now. Get that diploma and move the hell on." Evan runs his hand through his hair, looking irritated. The air of utter exhaustion that hangs over him is palpable and I wonder if he knows just how much I understand where he's at in life.

Because I'm right there with him, minus a sister to take care of. Instead there's a girl I want to take care of. A girl who means the fucking world to me. Maybe we can eventually share that duty or maybe we can't but for now, I'm going to try my best to respect his wishes.

No matter how hard that might end up being.

Chapter
EIGHTEEN

Dear Diary,

(November 14th, 3:09 a.m.) I haven't written anything in you in a long time. I almost threw you away because it's embarrassing to read my past entries, especially the last one when I was drunk and realizing that my life was nothing but a bunch of crap.

Worse are the even earlier ones. Before I realized what was happening to my family. How we were splintering apart. I was such a fool. So naïve and stupid, believing everything I saw and heard for my entire life. It was all a pack of lies. The only one who was ever one hundred percent honest with me was Evan.

And Nick. For the most part.

He's back in my life and I never thought that would happen. He walked so easily into my life and just as easily walked right on back out of it. I thought I did something wrong. I thought I somehow drove him away, made him fall out of love with me, and that hurt so much. Then I became angry and told myself I didn't love him either. It was just a foolish lack of judgment on my part. Caught up in a summer romance with a handsome boy, that could happen to any seventeen-year-old girl, right?

But then he shows up at my work and my entire body reacted like he never left. My semi-rational brain told me to get rid of him and I tried, though I really didn't want to. The way I feel about him confuses me. I want him but I shouldn't. I love him but he'll hurt me.

I don't like the back and forth. The uncertainty. The wondering. I wish it were simpler. But life isn't simple. I discovered that the hard way.

Nick is in my apartment now, at this very moment and knowing he's so close, I couldn't sleep. I couldn't resist him either, no matter how hard I tried, no matter how much I tried to convince myself that going to him would be the wrong thing to do.

Guess what? I went to him. I let him pull me onto his lap. I savored the feel of his strong arms around me, holding me close, my hands on his warm, firm skin, my mouth on his. The boy can kiss like no other and now that I have a few to compare him to there is just...no comparison.

I came to a realization while kissing him. One that clung to me long after I left him and went back to my room. It's why I finally dug out this old diary and decided to write in it again. I needed to get out my thoughts. My feelings.

I'm madly in love with him. I know it's stupid. I bet he'll break my heart again but I don't care. I'm throwing myself into this for however long it lasts and I'm going to enjoy every second of it.

So here I am, confessing my love for him once again. It never stopped. Like it could. All I want from him is more. More and more and more until there's nothing left for him to give. I want him to be mine.

All mine.

Evan will protest I'm sure but I don't care. He can't tell me what to do. I'll finish school and see Nick when I can. And the minute I graduate I'm moving. Or I'll convince Nick to move here. It sounds crazy because we're so young but Mom told me long, long ago that once you know, you know.

And I know. I'm convinced Nicholas Fairfield is the boy...the man for me.

No one is going to convince me otherwise.

Chapter
NINETEEN

November 14th

I wake up and practically jump out of bed, excited to see Nick splayed out on my couch, which is dumb, I know. I need to play this cool, not act like an overeager puppy ready to slobber all over him.

But I can't help it. Despite everything and how wary I still feel, I'm happy he's here. That Evan didn't kick him out. That I went back out to Nick after Evan went to bed and talked to him. Kissed him...

With as much calm as I can muster, I exit my bedroom, walking slowly down the hall like I'm some sort of regal princess parading for my royal subjects until I come to a stop in the middle of the living room. Only to discover the couch is empty, the blankets Nick used last night folded neatly and sitting on the coffee table, ready to be put away.

He's gone. Like he was never here last night. Glancing around, I look for a clue, a hint of something that he really was here, but there's nothing. Maybe I made it all up. The way we talked, how he kissed me...

False. A dream.

My knees weaken and I settle heavily on the couch before they completely give way. I've never been more disappointed in my life. Dipping my head, I bite my lip so hard I'm afraid I might make myself bleed and close my eyes, fighting back the tears.

He's just…gone.

"I sent him to go pick up coffee and doughnuts," Evan says from behind me.

I whirl around on a gasp, staring at the guy who just said the best sentence I've ever heard. "Why?" I ask, my voice a harsh whisper. Anger and relief war within me and I tell myself to let it go.

At least he's coming back.

"Because those are your two favorite things. I think he's become your third favorite thing, not that I approve. I have a feeling the kid is nothing but trouble." He rounds the couch and sits beside me.

"Evan," I start to protest but he shuts me off in that way he has. With the pointed glare and firm shake of his head I've become so accustomed to.

"I'm serious, Rev. I'll let you go with him to give that statement to the police. It's the right thing to do, I get that, but I don't want you spending too much time with him. You're too young to get all serious with a guy who's had zero chances in life. Walk away while you can."

His words are harsh. He's asking me to give up on someone I love. How can I do that? "What if I can't?" I whisper. "What if I don't want to?"

"You can and you have to," Evan says firmly. "The minute you're done giving your statement and cutting that poor guy a break, your butt is coming back here on a Greyhound bus. So you'll be home by late tonight, you got it? I already gave him cash to pay for your ticket. I'll pick you up at the bus station, just make sure you text me what time you're supposed to get there."

Evan has it all planned out and he didn't even tell me. When did he talk to Nick about this? Does he know what's going on? And Evan can't afford to pay for a stupid bus ticket, not that Nick can afford to drive me back and forth and then back again on his own. "Are you serious? That ticket must've cost too much…" I have no idea what a bus ticket costs but it had to have been pricey.

"It was cheap, don't worry." He moves from the couch lightning fast so he's kneeling in front of me, his face in mine, grim determination etched in his features. I stare at Evan, blinking at him, waiting for the speech that I know is coming. He's become a man in such a short amount of time and he's doing a bang up job of it. "You need to get in and get out quick. Nick seems all right but he's had some tough times. The kid never seems to catch a break."

"I'm trying to be the break he catches," I murmur, reaching out to grab Evan's hand and grip it tight. "I want to help him, not hurt him."

"Then help him with the statement and walk away. If you try and stick with him, this won't end well and you know it."

"You can't predict the future, Evan. You don't know how it'll end."

"How does everything else end for this kid, Rev? Like shit, that's how," he practically spits out, sounding angry. "In and out of jail, his mom dies, his ex-girlfriend is freaking murdered." I start to say something, shocked that he knows all about Nick, but he cuts me off with a stern look. "Yeah, I've done my research and he told me a few things. You've been dealing with nothing but shit lately and you're holding on to this guy like he could be your savior. Why, because he's kissed you a few times and rocked your world?"

I look away, immediately uncomfortable. No way am I answering that. My hot cheeks are probably answer enough.

"And I definitely don't want to know what you two have done because that's just disgusting. You're my sister." He shakes his head, dismissing that particular subject thankfully, and then he squeezes my hand, forcing me to meet his gaze once more. "I'm trying to protect you, Rev. Stay away from him. I know you think you're in love with him or whatever but it isn't going to work between you two. I know it."

They're all trying to protect me and it's so annoying. I sometimes wish they'd leave me alone. And how does he know it's not going to work with Nick and I? His saying that makes me want to prove him wrong.

"You don't know for sure," I tell him. "If I take your advice, we're doomed before we start."

"Aren't you already doomed? Think about it."

Evan leaves me to take a shower and I do think about it, pacing back and forth in the living room as I chew on my index finger. I think about it too much, Evan's words racing through my mind, filling me with doubt. Are we already doomed? I don't doubt my decision to help him with the police because I refuse to let him get caught up in that game again if I can put a stop to it. And I can. I'm his alibi and I won't let them harass him anymore.

But beyond that...should we continue to see each other? I don't know much about Nick, and what he's told me hasn't been a lot. We haven't known each other long. He's so sweet and patient with me. Our summer romance filled my heart with silly, overblown expectations I'm sure. I felt so connected to him, so convinced that we were meant to be together.

But is that enough? Everyone thinks we're young and stupid and they're probably right.

Muttering in frustration, I run to my bedroom and go to my dresser, pulling open the top drawer. I dig beneath my panties and bras to pull out the tiny rose-colored glass bottle, the one that Nick gave me for my birthday.

I stare at the label, the neatly printed "dreams" centered perfectly in the center. I had dreams. I believed in them too. They were taken from me, one after another over the last few months and I let that deter me. Nearly let it destroy me.

"Hey."

I glance up to find Nick standing in my bedroom doorway, one arm braced above him and gripping the wood frame. He looks good in a pair of charcoal gray sweats sitting low on his hips, his long-sleeved white T-shirt riding up a bit, displaying a sliver of his flat stomach. A shiver moves through me and I drop the bottle back into the drawer and shut it with a firm slam. "Hi," I say as I turn to face him completely.

"I brought breakfast." He doesn't enter my room, almost as if he's afraid to, and I go to him, my steps tentative, my mind turning over and over the discussion I had with Evan.

"I heard. Thank you." I stop just in front of him. He smells good. Looks even better. "Doughnuts?"

He nods, a faint smile curling his lips. He didn't shave this morning and there's a faint growth of stubble lining his jaw, tinged with gold. I want to rub my palm against his face. Press my cheek to his. But I restrain myself. "Evan says they're your favorite."

"My guilty pleasure." I could call him the same.

His smile grows. "I like that you actually have a guilty pleasure."

"Ha ha." I reach out to slug his shoulder but he's quicker than me, grabbing my wrist and pulling me into him. I brace my other hand on his chest, my fingers curling into his T-shirt and I lift my head to find his descending, his mouth drawing closer, closer…

His lips are on mine, soft and damp. I let him kiss me, a shiver stealing through my body when he lets go of my wrist to entwine our hands, lacing our fingers together as he delves his tongue deep inside my mouth. The kiss goes from sweet to hot in a matter of seconds and his arm tightens around my waist when I try to pull away.

I can't focus when he does that. And I think he knows it.

"I couldn't sleep last night," he whispers against my lips when we break apart. "All I could think about was you."

"Nick," I start but he kisses me again, silencing me. His magical kisses won't let me forget what I wanted to say though.

I just choose not to say it. Classic avoidance technique, but I don't want to face reality right now. I don't think he wants to either.

We go to the kitchen and I flip open the lid of the giant pink box that's sitting on the counter, grabbing a maple bar and plopping it on a napkin. Evan joins us minutes later, fresh out of his shower and dressed for work.

"I think you should call into work," my brother suggests casually right before he sinks his teeth into a chocolate frosted doughnut.

I'm shocked. Since we've been on our own, we've never called in sick to our jobs. We need every hour—and every dollar that hour brings—that we can get. "Are you serious?"

He shrugs and takes a sip from the to-go cup of coffee Nick brought him. "It's going to be a long day for you. The faster you get back up there and give your statement to the police, the faster it's all done."

Ugh. I know what he means, but Evan can be so rude sometimes. I send him a look, wishing he would shut up so he doesn't hurt Nick's feelings.

"I think you should too," Nick says, settling onto the barstool right next to mine. "I agree with your brother. The faster we get this handled, the better. There's a storm brewing out there too you know."

"There is?" A shiver races down my spine and I wonder if he's being literal or referring to something else. There have been lots of storms brewing lately, all around me. Some of them even I created.

Evan leaps up and goes to the front window, jerking open the blinds, allowing the weak morning light to filter in. The sky outside is unusually dark and foreboding, the wind blowing through the bare trees, rocking their branches almost violently. "Hell yeah, there is." He turns to study us, his brows lowered, a frown on his face. "Maybe you should wait it out."

Ah, my worried brother. I still marvel at how much he's changed in such a short amount of time. I guess responsibility does that to a person. "Make up your mind," I tease him. "Either we stay or we go."

"We should definitely go," Nick says firmly as his gaze meets mine for the briefest second before he returns his attention to Evan, who walks back to the counter and grabs his doughnut. "She can call in to her work, we'll get on the road and take care of this."

"Just…be careful. I bet traffic will be for shit and the road conditions bad," Evan says, shoving the last of his doughnut into his mouth before he reaches into the box and grabs another one. "I hate driving in the rain and dealing with idiots who speed."

"You should hear yourself right now," I say, barely repressing the laugh that wants to escape. Once upon a time he was the idiot who was always speeding. "You sound like an old man."

"Shit's changed, Rev," he says, his voice sounding downright…dire. Sometimes I miss my cocky, jerkwad brother. Only because I miss how carefree he used to be. Now the weight of the world is always on his shoulders. "You know this better than anyone."

"I'm not worried," I say, waving my hand. "The weather keeps lying anyway. None of the storms that have come through have amounted to much."

"The sky is pretty damn dark," Evan points out, his attention going to Nick. "Don't drive like a total jackass. Think of my sister."

"I'm always thinking of your sister," Nick says with complete sincerity.

My heart swells at his words. "Stop trying to scare him," I chastise Evan.

"He's not trying to scare me," Nick reassures me, resting his hand over mine. "He's just worried about you."

They are all worried about me and I both appreciate their concern and want them to knock it off. Fine, I've acted like a simpering baby most of my life, but how can I grow and spread my wings if they're constantly trying to hold me back?

"We'll be fine." I smile brightly but it feels oddly false. "Everything will be just fine."

Chapter
TWENTY

Two p.m., longest day ever

The tension in the air of my truck cab is thick. Reverie and I have hardly spoken since we left her apartment and at first, I figured she was just worried about the weather.

Because Evan was right, it's for shit. The moment we pulled onto the freeway the skies opened up and dumped rain on us. So heavy it became hard to see and traffic slowed to a crawl. Probably safer but frustrating as hell.

We've been on the road for almost two hours and we're almost there, thank Christ. I'm anxious, feeling antsy after concentrating on the road for so long, and I'm dying to get out and stretch my legs.

Her silence is starting to freak me out. Is she having regrets? What if she doesn't tell the cops the truth after all? Not that I think she'd come all this way just to screw me over but…

I don't know. After dealing with Krista for so long it's hard for me to wrap my brain around a girl wanting to actually help me, I guess.

We kissed when I came back from making the breakfast run but other than that, there's been no real affection happening between us. She's sitting in her seat and I'm sitting in mine and the space between us feels long. Like miles, oceans, galaxies long. She's got her arms crossed

92

in front of her and her face averted as she stares out the window, her gaze locked on the ocean as we pass by it.

The water is gray and swirling, capped white and turbulent. The storm is stirring everything up including my thoughts and I can hardly fucking stand it.

"Are you mad at me?" I finally ask, unable to take it anymore.

She turns to look at me, her arms still crossed in front of her chest, her expression incredulous. Relief trickles through my veins but I'm cautious until I hear her answer. "Why would you ask that?"

I shrug, feeling stupid for asking. "You've hardly talked to me."

"You've hardly talked to me," she returns.

A frustrated chuckle escapes me. "Driving in this shit weather is doing a number on me I guess."

"And knowing I have to talk to the police and answer their questions is making me nervous," she says softly. "It has nothing to do with you. I'm not mad at you." She pauses. "Are you mad at me?"

"Hell, no," I say vehemently. "I'm grateful you're doing this for me."

"I'm not doing anything but telling the truth." Another pause, this one longer before she says, "Why did you not let me see you when I came by the jail?"

I withhold the frustrated sigh that wants to stream out of me. "I…I didn't want you to see me like that."

"Like what? Like an innocent man being held against his will?"

"Now you're just being dramatic," I retort but damn it, her words stick with me because she's right.

"No, I'm really not. Your refusing to see me broke my heart, Nick. I thought…I thought you hated me or that you were mad at me when I didn't do anything. I—I don't know, it was all so crazy around then and I didn't understand what was happening."

"I've said it before and I'll say it again until you finally get it. I was trying to *protect* you. I didn't want the cops to find out you were with me because of who you are, Reverie. You're the daughter of a famous televangelist. They would've splashed my scandal all over the news and dragged you along with me."

"But at least you wouldn't have been a suspect any longer," she says.

"Yeah, but your reputation would've been ruined."

"My reputation was already ruined because of what my parents did. No one wants to talk to the Hales unless they can find out some juicy gossip. My mom spoke to the media at first because she was trying so hard to portray herself as the victim but after realizing all they were doing was vilifying her, she gave up." Reverie shakes her head. "You tried to protect me for nothing, Nick. I hope you realize that."

"Am I supposed to feel bad about that?" I ask, chancing a glance in her direction to find her studying me.

"I don't know," she says with a little shrug.

Damn. Females. They make no sense to me, even the ones I love.

I pull into town not fifteen minutes later and I head straight for the police station, not wanting to waste any time. Now I'm the one left confused. I don't know what Reverie wants from me and I'm almost afraid to ask because I might not want to hear her answer. The push and pull going on between us is aggravating to say the least.

My conversation with Evan earlier this morning repeats in my head, no matter how hard I try to banish it.

She's too young.

You're too young.

She's still in high school.

She has so much potential.

You live in a different city.

You come from two different worlds.

She has enough to deal with.

And so do you.

Your summer fling was meaningless. You both just got...caught up.

I protested only the last reason because what happened between Reverie and I over the summer was the farthest thing from meaningless. But whatever. Evan's never been in love. He doesn't know what it's like.

"Is this okay?" I ask after I park the truck in front of the station. The rain is still coming down hard, hitting the windshield with rhythmic force, and she peers up at the imposing building in front of us, squinting. "That we came here first?"

"Yeah." She presses her lips together. "I hope I say the right thing."

"Just tell them the truth. That's all they want to hear."

"That detective wasn't very nice."

"He's just pissed because he'd love to pin Krista's murder on me." That they have no other suspects makes me think Krista's killer might've done this before. She hung out with all kinds of shady characters, especially the last few months of her life. It could've been anyone.

But it definitely wasn't me.

"Does he hate you that much?"

"He just doesn't have any other suspect. What they really hate is having an open murder case that they can't solve. The town doesn't like it either, imagining a murderer walking their streets." Something I have close experience with. I've been considered a murderer in not just one but *two* separate cases.

I really need to get the hell out of this town.

"I can't say that I blame them. But it's not right that they seem to always blame you either." Reverie shivers. "I don't like how much it makes me sad, being here. It's so different during the winter. Dark and cold and dreary."

"Not always." It's brighter now that she's here with me but I don't say that. She'd probably just roll her eyes and tell me to stop anyway. "But yeah. It's a different town when summer's over and the tourists leave."

"Michael left too, right? Do you still talk to him?" She flashes me a smile. "I miss him. He's so goofy. He always made me laugh."

"I do talk to him. We text a lot." He's coming home for Thanksgiving and I'll be glad to see him. "He's doing good."

"How about Heather? Is he still with her?"

"Nah. That relationship ended the minute summer was over." Michael hadn't been too broken up about it. He'd known what he was dealing with going in—a summer fling, pure and simple.

Her smile fades. "Do you regret last summer and everything that happened?"

She's changing subjects so quick I can hardly keep up. I scoot closer to her and grab her hands, squeezing them tight. "No. I don't regret meeting you. I don't regret spending time with you. I don't regret any part of you, Reverie. The only thing I regret is what happened to Krista and how that...ruined us."

We're silent for a while as we absorb what I said. Krista's death did ruin us but I wonder if we were doomed to fail from the beginning.

"You and me...we're not a good idea, are we?" she finally asks.

I release one of her hands and cup her cheek, tilting her head up so our mouths are almost perfectly aligned. "Probably not. But that's not going to stop me from trying for us again."

She closes her eyes, the corners of her mouth tilting upward. "You say the sweetest things, I swear."

I kiss her, keeping it brief because it would be so easy to get carried away. I refuse to make out with her in the parking lot of the police station so I tell her we should make a run for it and get inside as fast as possible. We both jerk up the hoods on our sweatshirts and climb out of the truck, running through the pouring rain as we dodge the various puddles heading toward the front entrance.

It's a Saturday afternoon and with the shitty weather, no one is really around. The streets in town were pretty much abandoned too because unlike the citizens of southern California, who are driving everywhere at all times, the people in my small town batten down the hatches and stay inside when it storms like this.

I'd rather be anywhere other than this place, which is full of nothing but bad memories. I've spent far too much time at a police station—in freaking *jail*—for someone my age. I tell myself I can't regret what's happened to me because spending time here wouldn't have led me to Reverie but...

Yeah. I regret it. I was wronged and no one seemed to care. I can't let that fuel my actions for the rest of my life but I certainly have a right to be bitter.

And man, I hate being inside the station, the familiar smell, the sounds, the drab color of the walls. I'm right back where I don't want to be and am thankful that the moment Reverie is done giving her statement, I can walk my ass out of here and never look back.

If I were smart and had an actual plan, I'd leave this town for good. I have a decent job but I can find one just like it anywhere. I can find an apartment and new friends too. I don't need this place.

But change is hard. I have no one to rely on.

Only me.

We approach the front desk and Reverie asks to see Detective Jacoby. The man appears within seconds of receiving notice we're here and he leads the both of us back to his desk, holding his hand out toward the two chairs in front of it, indicating he wants us to sit down.

"You wasted no time getting here," he says to Reverie with a pleasant smile. But I can see the disappointment in his gaze. I know he doesn't like that I'm here with her. This guy has never been on my side and my alibi is going to disappoint him.

"I figured I needed to get this over with. So you would leave Nick alone once and for all," she says, fidgeting in her seat. I can tell she's uncomfortable and I wish I could give her hand a reassuring squeeze but I don't. We need to remain as neutral as possible, especially in front of this guy.

"So you're the one who brought her here?" Jacoby settles his attention on me.

"I gave her ride, yeah." I nod.

"Nasty weather out there." He points out the obvious. "Guess it was worth it though, to get us off your ass, right?" Jacoby laughs at his own joke, though Reverie and I both don't even crack a smile.

Jerk. He's making fun of my *life*. A life the police force have made miserable going on almost two years.

He sobers up real quick. "All right, little lady. Let's get you settled so we can record your statement." Standing, he hitches up his pants, keeping his gaze pinned on her. "You ready?"

She blinks up at him. "You're not going to question me here?"

"Nah, it's too noisy out here with everyone around. And we gotta get rid of Fairfield." Jacoby jerks a thumb in my direction. "Can't have him lurking around sending you looks, getting you to change your statement if you say something wrong."

I'm offended and from what I can tell, so is Reverie. She stands, her head held high. Jacoby is a complete dumbass. "He can't change the *truth*, Detective Jacoby. I don't like how you imply he has control over what I'm going to say."

"Why, I never said any such thing," he blusters, his cheeks ruddy.

"You implied it though and that's almost the same thing." She straightens her shoulders, her expression cool and composed, completely unruffled. Yet again, I'm impressed as hell. Jacoby most likely can sense he won't rattle her and I bet he hates that. "Are you ready?"

"I am." He leads her away, sending me a long, measured look as he glances over his shoulder one last time. I return the same look, refusing to let him intimidate me.

I stare at them long after they disappear out of vision, the relief that takes hold of me so strong I almost want to shout with happiness. This is it. They can't come after me any longer. I'm done with this place.

So. Done.

I'm making my way out of the room where the other detectives' desks are when I hear someone shuffle up behind me.

"Well, look at you. Finally come down to the station to confess your sins and tell everyone what you did to my sweet little girl?"

All the relief bleeds out of me until I feel as flat as a deflated balloon. I recognize that voice. He sounds drunk. Angry. Frustrated.

Slowly I turn to find Krista's father standing in front of me, wavering on his feet, his eyes bloodshot, his mouth turned up in one corner with a sneer. She looked so much like him, though prettier, of course. She was mean when she drank too.

Just like her dad.

"Hey Mr. Benson," I offer in greeting because I don't know what else to say, waiting for the blow of his words pummeling me. The man likes to shout. I've heard him do it enough. I don't think being inside a police station will stop him either.

"Don't you 'hey' me, you stupid little fucker," he mutters, stepping closer to me. I take a step back, wrinkling my nose at the strong scent of alcohol I smell on his breath. "Why are you here? Did they finally find something to pin this on you? Because we all know you did it. You killed my Krista."

"I didn't do it, sir," I start but he interrupts me, cutting me off.

"*Sir.*" He spits the word out, like it's a curse. "Aren't you cute, trying to be all respectable and shit." He grabs hold of the front of my shirt and jerks me close to him, his face in mine. "Give it up and tell the truth, boy. Tell them once and for all what you did to my girl and maybe then God can forgive you. Because I know I sure as hell can't."

He's gonna hit me. Choke me. Something, I don't know what, but he's pissed off and looking for a fight. His fingers tighten on my shirt, pulling me even closer to him and I glance around, shocked but not really that no one is paying us any mind.

Fucking cops would probably love to see Krista's dad beat the shit out of me. They'd probably call it poetic justice because in their eyes, I'm guilty.

Jesus, what sort of corrupt town do I live in anyway?

"Let him go, Hal. Before the cops arrest your ass for assault."

Hal lets me go at the same time I look to my right to find of all people David standing there, a grim expression on his face. I brush off the front of my sweatshirt, backing away from both of them.

"What the hell are you doing here?" I ask incredulously. My old friend looks the same but he doesn't. There's a weariness clinging to him, as if he's given up on this town, on himself. There's an edginess to him too, as he bounces on his feet, back and forth, almost like he's looking for a fight.

Great.

"We come here a lot to talk to the detectives who are working on the investigation," David explains. "See if they have any new leads into Krista's murder."

Well, no shit. Look at my former best friend, helping my ex's dad find her murderer. Talk about twisted. "I didn't realize you and Hal were so close."

"We became close after what...happened," David says like it's no big deal.

Uh huh. This doesn't sit right. Can't explain why but what the hell is David really doing? Not that I can trust the fucker or his motives and that's probably my biggest problem. This all smells wrong to me. Looks wrong. Feels wrong.

And usually when I feel like this, I need to trust my instincts.

"He's helped me a lot more than you ever did, you little shit," Hal adds. Trying to get a rise out of me I'm sure but I refuse to take the bait.

Bad enough, how weird it is to have David here, perfectly calm and acting like it's normal to hang out in a police station all the time. He did more jail time than I did so you'd think he wouldn't want to step near this place once he got out.

"You all right, buddy?" David asks, a faint smile on his face. Like we're back to being best friends again or something. "What are you doing here anyway?"

"Confessing his sins is what I told him. He needs to come clean," Hal says. David sends him a look and Hal clamps his lips shut tight.

"He's been…upset that there's been no progress in the investigation," David tells me, like Hal isn't standing right next to us. "He's been drinking heavily, especially lately."

More like he's been drinking heavily since we were little kids but I let it slide. "Not much evidence in the case, huh?"

"Not enough, and the police aren't saying much either. Whoever did it knew what he was doing." David leans in closer when he says that last bit, like he doesn't want Krista's dad to hear. Good call. "We're starting to wonder if it was someone from out of town. A stranger passing through."

"Maybe." I scratch my chin, wishing I could get the hell out of here. Given the chance, I'll leave the building and wait out in my truck for Reverie. Text her where I'm am so she doesn't think I bailed.

I can't stand it in here already. And it's become a million times worse dealing with these two from my not so distant past.

"So why are you here?" David asks, his tone pleasant, as is his expression. He's dressed in jeans and a button down plaid shirt, looking every inch a respectable teenage boy hanging out at the police station waiting for more information about a killer. His look, the way he's acting, none of it rings true for me. It feels like an act and I wonder if I'm the only one not falling for it.

"My uh, friend is talking to the cops," I offer, not wanting to explain myself any further.

David frowns. "What friend?"

"You don't know her."

"Is it that girl who's family you were working for?" At my look of surprise David continues on. "Krista told me all about her."

Shit. That means he must know about the trouble Krista tried to cause between us too. "What exactly did she tell you?"

"Nothing important." He waves a hand, dismissing my question. "What's done is done. Though I'm wondering what she could possibly say to the detectives that would matter to the investigation."

"She's giving a statement as to my whereabouts regarding the night Krista was murdered," I explain further, fighting against the panic that's rising within me. I don't like this, making small talk with my backstabbing ex-best friend. I'm desperate to get out of here.

"Your whereabouts? What are you saying?" Hal asks, his voice getting louder, if that's possible. "Is she claiming she was with you that night?"

"She *was* with me." Anger fills me and I turn to walk away, tossing over my shoulder. "I don't have to explain myself to you. I didn't kill Krista. Take your rage out on someone else."

I start to leave the building and David follows after me like a loyal dog, calling my name. I refuse to look at him, acknowledge him, but he grabs hold of my arm and stops me just in front of the station entrance.

"I'm sorry, man. You have to understand where he's coming from. He's upset they don't have a firm suspect," David says. "Well, except for you."

My hands clench into fists like I have no control over them. "I'm not a suspect. I have an alibi."

His brows rise. "All of a sudden, huh? That's…interesting."

"It's the truth."

"Funny how the supposed truth comes out months after Krista dies." David steps closer, his pleasant, easygoing demeanor evaporating in a second. He glowers at me, his stance downright menacing and I wonder if he picked up this shift in mood while he was in jail. You learn from the best there. A real first hand lesson on criminal behavior.

"Go ahead and say what you want to say, David." I take a step away, leaning against the wall, hands shoved in my pockets but my fists still clenched. I could take him out quick. At least, I used to be able to. He's bigger now, though not as tall as me. And he might've learned a few moves in jail too. "I can tell you're just dying to get it out."

He smirks, his gaze cold. "Just get it over with and tell them you did it, Nick. They all suspect you. We all know you killed her. She was driving you crazy, unable to take no for an answer and nagging at you all the time. You finally couldn't take it anymore."

I can't believe the nerve of this asshole. "Is that how you think it played out?"

"Sure." He shrugs, the smirk still firmly planted on his face. I want to punch it off, again and again until he's swollen and bleeding. Fucker. "Krista was always persistent. A real pain in the ass, but also a good lay, right? So you could look past her crazy behavior just to get with her. At least, I could."

He's trying to provoke me on purpose but I remain silent, refusing to say something stupid and give him ammunition to use against me.

"I know she was trying to blackmail you to dump your rich little girlfriend." At my non-reaction he laughs. "You're good with that poker face but I see you're surprised I know. She told me everything. She was so frustrated you didn't want her anymore that she turned to me. And trust me, I tried to convince her to leave you alone but she wouldn't listen to me."

"Right. I'm sure you were working her over, trying to win her back," I retort. "I don't need to hear this shit, David. I don't care what you two did together. I didn't kill her. I didn't see her that night. I don't know what happened or who did that to her."

"You were supposed to meet her."

"And I didn't. I was with Reverie."

He narrows his eyes. "Right. Reverie, the rich girlfriend Krista hated. Such a stupid name, but I heard she's a real brainless twit so there's that." Another reluctant laugh slips from him. "The sweet and pure minister's daughter. Did it make you feel better, fucking a virgin? Was it worth it? Considering she's not rich anymore, I don't see how it could've worked out too well for you since you didn't gain much. Though that alibi she's currently giving you must be worth something."

I rush him without thought, grabbing hold of his shirt and tossing him hard against the wall. "I should kick your ass for saying that about her," I mutter.

"Go ahead and try. I know how to put up a fight," David says, his words full of bravado but his eyes edged with fear. "Such a big reaction, dude. Truth hurts, or something along those lines, right? Be glad you've covered your tracks with this chick. Your luck will run out eventually."

"You're an asshole." I release my hold on him and step away, watching with satisfaction as he sags against the wall, reaching up to brush the wrinkles out of his shirt front. "Not worth me getting in trouble for beating your ass."

"Fuck off," David says, glaring at me. "They'll find out the truth. They'll realize you're the one who killed Krista and I'll make sure of it. I'm the only one who really cares about that girl. Everyone else tossed her aside like trash, even her father."

"What, are you saying you're the only one who loved her?" Please. He's the most selfish asshole I know.

"More than you ever did, that's for damn sure. Enjoy your freedom, Fairfield. It won't last long," he calls after me as I start to walk away.

"Fuck you," I mutter under my breath, pushing through the front entrance of the police station and walking out into the rain. The cold air wraps around me, stealing the oxygen from my lungs, and I tip my head back, closing my eyes as the raindrops sting my skin as they fall.

The last thing I need is David chasing after me for the rest of my life, hell-bent on proving I murdered Krista. He's the kind of dick that would do just that, terrorizing my ass despite all the evidence thrown at him proving I didn't do it.

I gotta get out of here. I have some money saved. I could give notice on my apartment, sell a few of mom's things that I don't need and put the rest in storage, quit my job, box up my shit and go. I can't take this town anymore. The looks people give me, the whispers. I'm innocent but I may as well be guilty.

But where do I go?

Chapter
TWENTY-ONE

4 p.m.

Detective Jacoby kept me in that stuffy little room for over an hour, asking me endless questions after I gave my statement, repeating many of them like he was trying to catch me in a lie, which he probably was.

Whatever. I kept my composure the entire time, explaining myself again and again. Even answering the uncomfortable questions as neutrally as possible, though I could feel my cheeks flame with embarrassment constantly.

You were with him all night? Where exactly? In his bed?

Were the two of you having sex, Miss Hale?

Did he ever leave you alone in the middle of the night?

Do you think he killed Krista Benson?

How long have you two been involved?

Was he carrying on a relationship with you while also engaging in sexual activity with Krista?

Do you trust him, Miss Hale? Really?

Over and over, the same types of questions worded in different ways but I always answered the same. It felt like it went on forever and I was exhausted despite the giant cup of coffee he gave me to help keep me focused.

Finally he let me go, offering a gruff thank you as his goodbye, his expression full of disappointment as he escorted me out of the police station and practically pushed me into the lobby. He left me there without another word and I stood alone, checking my phone for a text from Nick since he was nowhere to be seen.

I'm waiting for you in my truck. Couldn't take it in there anymore.

Breathing a sigh of relief, I push my way through the glass double doors and out into the rain, yanking my hood up as I make a run for Nick's truck. It's parked in the same spot. I see him sitting inside, the windows steamy from his breathing, his head leaning back against the seat like he's trying to take a nap.

I'm so happy to see him I run through the puddles, splashing water and getting my jeans wet along with my shoes. But I don't care. Without thought I open the passenger side door and leap into the truck, throwing myself at him.

"Hey, hey." He springs up, sounding sleepy as his arms automatically go around me. I'm shaking as I bury my face against his warm neck, breathing deep his delicious, soapy clean scent. He brushes the hood from my head, his fingers tangling in my hair. "What's wrong? You okay?"

"I'm just glad it's over." I kiss his neck, forgetting my earlier promise to myself that we wouldn't do this. That I would walk away from him as soon I left the police station.

I don't care what Evan says. The last thing I want is to walk away from Nick. "I felt like Jacoby was trying to trick me."

"Because he probably was. You're ruining his investigation in his eyes." His fingers jerk in my hair when I kiss his neck again and his reaction fuels me. I rain a trail of kisses up the length of his throat, along his jaw, his chin…

"Hey." He grabs my shoulders and pulls me away from him slightly so he can look at me. "Are you okay?"

I shake my head, desperation clawing at my insides, making my heart race, my head spin. "Take me back to your place."

Nick frowns. "I thought I was supposed to take you to the bus station."

He's still trying to stick by his promise to my brother when I've just abandoned it. It's like we can't ever get on the same page. Should I take that as a sign? "My bus doesn't leave for hours. Please, Nick. Don't make me sit down there and wait around for it. Let's go hang out at your place."

He looks so unsure of my plan and I hate that. "Do you want to get something to eat first?"

I shake my head again, frustrated that he's trying to deter me. "No. Don't worry about what Evan's going to think. He's not here. He can't tell me what to do." I reach for him, my fingers curling in his sweatshirt. "Please, Nick. I'm begging you."

He contemplates me for so long I'm afraid he's going to tell me no. "Okay," he finally says with a sigh. "We'll go to my apartment, we'll have something to eat and then I'm taking you to the bus station. I'll wait with you until your bus comes, okay? I won't leave you alone there, I swear. I promised Evan I would get you on that bus and get you home safely."

"Okay." I nod, my mind filling with all the possibilities. This feels like my last chance with him. I don't know why but the uneasy sensation weighs heavy on my heart, my soul. I'm so afraid he's going to do what my brother wants and walk away from me. I'm supposed to walk away from him too but being with him again like this makes me realize I don't want to. I want another chance.

And I'm not going to give up until I can convince him we deserve another chance. The two of us together. We just need to get out of this crappy small town, away from where everything bad happened. It's so strange, but I didn't have this sense of foreboding back at my apartment like I do here. There's a tension vibrating off of Nick's body and I don't understand it. All I can think is that he hates this town so much he can hardly stand being here.

We drive back to his place slowly, Nick cautious as he navigates the streets, doing his best to avoid the flooded spots that pop up here and there. I grip the handle on the inside of the passenger side door, my fingers so tight my knuckles are white. I don't know why I feel so anxious, so apprehensive.

All I know is that I need Nick.

The second he parks the truck, we burst out of it, running to his apartment in the heavy rain. I chase after him, following him inside, and when he shuts and locks the door, I'm all over him like I can't control myself. He buries his hands in my hair, gripping either side of my head and holding me firm, staring at me as if he can't quite believe I'm there. And then he's kissing me. His lips are hungry and persuasive, his tongue stroking against mine, wet and hot and tempting me to want more. I moan, a desperate, needy sound as I claw at his front, my hands diving beneath his sweatshirt, flipping under his T-shirt to touch bare, hot skin.

He flinches at my touch, his answering groan spurring me on, and we fall onto the couch, tangled up in each other, his knee firm between my legs, pressing against the ache that's building fast. I want him so bad and I want him to want me too. It's been too long since I've been with him like this and I've missed him so much.

Does he know what he does to me? How out of control he makes me feel?

"Reverie." His voice breaks through my lust-clouded thoughts but he doesn't stop me. I'm on top of him, tugging on his clothes, trying to undo his jeans. He clamps his hands on my shoulders, giving me a little shake, and I look into his eyes, blinking him into focus. "Revi. Slow down, baby."

The sweet nickname he has for me stops me and I lift away from him slightly, feeling dizzy. I remember when he used to called me Daydream but I think I like Revi better. "It's just…it's been so long," I whisper. "And I'm…." My voice drifts and I let my head fall forward, feeling stupid for getting so carried away.

He brushes the wayward strands of hair from my face and I lift my head to find him watching me, his expression gentle, his touch even more so. I want to melt into him. Become one with him and never leave his side. It's so crazy, my feelings for Nick. We've known each other for only a short time but that doesn't seem to matter.

All I know is that I care for him and want to be with him in every way possible.

"You're what?" he asks, tracing my face with his fingertips. I close my eyes as he touches my eyebrows, the slope of my nose, the curve of my lips.

"I'm scared," I say, my voice trembling, and I open my eyes. He drops his hand away from my face. "I don't like it here, Nick. And I don't like that you're here all alone, with no one to help you or protect you. In the summer, everything was different. It was bright and full of promise and sweet and fun. But now it's just…it's ugly. Dark and cold and depressing. Everyone acts like they're out to get you and I don't understand why." I cling to him, grabbing hold of his wrist, stopping him from touching me because I can't think when he touches me.

"It's not that bad," he starts but I shake my head, silencing him.

"It's awful and you know it. I don't know how you can stay here with them always following you, waiting for you to slip up," I say, resting my hands on his cheeks, cradling his face. I stare into his eyes, overwhelmed with my feelings for him. He's so precious to me and I don't think he even knows it. "You need to come back home with me."

"I can't. You know I can't," he whispers, his voice harsh, his eyes as dark as the storm outside. "Your brother doesn't want me there. He doesn't even want us together. And I have my job, my apartment. Mom's stuff is still in her room. I haven't even been able to go through it all yet. It'll take time. I need to plan. And I just…I have ties here, Reverie. I can't just pack up and leave."

"What about your ties to me? Do those exist?" I'm asking too much, I'm sure of it, but I have to know how he feels. If I'm important enough to him that he'll leave everything just for me.

You're being totally unfair.

I know it but I can't help myself.

He blows out a harsh breath and closes his eyes briefly. His agonized expression cracks my heart. "You know they do. I fell for you so fast, Reverie. It's fucking crazy, how much I feel for you. But it's just…it's not that easy for me to leave this place. I have nothing. No one who can help me and I don't want to burden you with that. Besides, you have your own life to live. You haven't even graduated high school yet. We can't expect this to work out between us. We're being totally unrealistic."

"I don't think we're being unrealistic." I'm also in complete denial. That I'm even aware of it is almost laughable.

"Give me a break," he says with a little frustrated laugh, shaking his head. "We need to be real with each other. I want this to work. You mean everything to me. But…I just, I don't know. Maybe we should wait."

I withdraw from his arms, a cold, dark pit forming in my stomach. "You think we should wait? Why?"

"You know exactly why. Our circumstances aren't ideal. And your brother thinks it's a bad idea."

"I really don't care what Evan thinks." I pause. Amazing how the words are true when I say them out loud. "Do you think it's a bad idea? Us together?"

Nick says nothing but I guess that's answer enough.

Lifting my chin, I climb off the couch and grab my purse, then make my way to the front door. "I should go."

He leaps from the couch and runs after me, slamming his hand flat against the door to prevent me from opening it. "You're not going

107

anywhere," he says, his voice firm, allowing me no argument. I've never seen him act so bossy. "Don't be stupid."

"Are you saying you think I'm stupid?" I turn on him, furious.

"If you're referring to you leaving this apartment in the rain with no form of transportation to get home then yes, I think you're *being* stupid." He grabs hold of my shoulders and turns me fully toward him, giving me a little shake. "Don't act like this. You know what I'm saying makes sense. You're just in denial."

I glare at him, hating that he's right and that he's able to read my mind. Hating that we shouldn't stay together no matter how much I want it to. Hating more that he feels the same way. The desperation overwhelms me, pushing me to be daring, to ask him for what I really want, no matter how hard it's going to be to actually say it. "Give me one more time then," I say.

He frowns, looking confused. "One more time, what?"

I roll my eyes, trying to let go of my embarrassment. We've been together before. He's seen me naked. I've bared my very soul to him. "I want to be with you, Nick." I touch his chest, my palm pressed against the center where I can feel his rapidly beating heart.

The sexy little smile that curls his lips makes my heart beat even faster than his. "Yeah?"

"Yes. The two of us. Together." I move into him, pressing my body close to his, not above using his attraction for me to get what I want. Because he wants it too, no matter how much he's protesting. "Give us that for the next couple of hours at least."

His breathing picks up and he parts his lips, staring down at me. "We shouldn't."

I stand on tiptoe and kiss his neck, just behind his ear, exactly where he likes it. A little shiver moves through him and I smile, pleased that I can make him react so easily. "You know you want to," I whisper.

The shuddering breath that escapes him when I slip my hands beneath his shirt and touch his stomach tells me that I've won this battle.

Now all I need is to win the war.

I'm dozing off in Nick's arms, our bodies entwined, my head nestled in that comfortable spot between his neck and shoulder when my cell phone dings, indicating I have a text.

"I should get that," I murmur, my eyes still closed. I don't ever want to leave this spot.

"No, you shouldn't." Nick's drifting his fingers up and down the length of my arm, drawing a circle on my shoulder, and his touch makes me smile. "Whoever it is, they can wait."

"What if it's Evan?" He's the only one who would text me, beyond Vanessa or Valerie and on extremely rare occasions, Tally. Up to a few weeks ago she was still interested in getting me to come and party with her, not that I ever did.

"He'll call you if it's important." Nick taps my shoulder twice, his touch firm. Opening my eyes, I glance up at him to find him watching me. "What happened to your phone anyway?"

I frown. "What are you talking about?"

"After you left town, I tried to text you but I never heard back. I thought you were ignoring me."

I had no idea. Why this excites me when that was months ago, I'm not sure. I guess the admission proves he still cared when I'd always believed he gave up on us. "I never got them. Our phones were taken away from us because they were funded through The Flock of the Lambs. When the assets were frozen, they took everything. We had to start over." I look away, resuming my position on Nick's shoulder. "Evan got phones for the both of us and I have a new number. Of course, you already know that since I gave it to you." I'd sent him a text for that intent last night and he'd updated me in his contacts list.

"You don't plan on getting rid of that phone anytime soon, do you?" he asks.

I slowly shake my head, nuzzling closer, my mouth right at his neck. I love to kiss him there. I love to kiss him everywhere. His skin is so smooth and warm. His entire body is perfect. I wish I could explore it for hours, not just these few stolen moments before he has to take me to the bus station. "Evan and I are in a two-year contract so we're stuck."

Nick chuckles, holding me closer. "Good. Because I don't want to lose contact with you again like that." He presses his lips against my forehead, giving me a lingering kiss, and warmth spreads through me, making me languid. Sleepy. I've never felt so happy.

Ever.

I'm almost asleep, I can tell Nick already is, when my cell starts to ring, the sound sharp in the otherwise quiet of the room. With a frustrated growl I withdraw from his arms and grab my phone off the bedside table, seeing that it is indeed my brother calling.

I so don't want to talk to him.

"What?" I mumble into the phone as I crawl out of bed and hide myself away in Nick's bathroom, where I catch my reflection when I switch on the light. I'm wearing one of his oversized T-shirts, my hair is a disaster and my lips are swollen. I look like a mess. More like I look like I've just had sex.

"Nice greeting," Evan says, sounding put out. "Are you already at the bus station?"

"Um, not yet." I comb my fingers through my hair, trying to straighten it but it's an absolute mess. I should just throw it into a ponytail or a topknot and forget about it.

"Where the hell are you then?"

"Nick's apartment." I bite my lip, waiting for his reply.

As expected, he explodes. "That is the last place you should be. Damn it, Rev, stop wasting your time and go catch that damn bus. The weather is bad, travel everywhere is delayed and the freeways are a mess. I just caught the news while I was on break and had to call you."

"We're leaving in a few minutes for the station," I reassure him.

"You need to be on that bus in less than an hour," he points out.

"We're going soon, I swear. The bus I'm supposed to take is probably not even there yet," I argue. "I'm guessing it'll show up late. Maybe I should wait and take a bus home tomorrow? Should the weather be cleared up by then?"

"The ticket is transferrable," Evan mutters. "But I want you home tonight."

Translation: He wants me to get away from Nick now.

"I'll go to the station and let you know what's happening, okay? Circumstances might be out of my control." I hope they are. I might even force them to be because I don't want to leave. Not yet. I want to spend the night with Nick. If I let the fear get to me, I could almost think this is my one last night with him for good.

But I refuse to do that. I need to believe that this is going to work out between us.

"Text me and let me know what's going on," Evan says. "And let me know what time your bus is scheduled to get in here. I'll make sure and be there to pick you up."

"You better be," I joke, wanting to lighten the mood. I don't want him mad or thinking the worst about Nick. I want the two most important men in my life to like each other and get along.

"Did you get to make your statement to the police?" Evan asks.

"I did. It went all right. I think they'll leave Nick alone now." I frown when I hear a noise coming from the other side of the door and then there's a light knock. I crack open the door to find Nick on the other side, his hair mussed, his eyes heavy. He's wearing boxer briefs and nothing else and he looks good enough to eat.

"You all right?" he whispers, scratching his bare chest.

My gaze tracks his hand's every movement. I wish I was touching him instead of talking to my pissed off brother. "It's Evan," I tell him. With an understanding nod, Nick pulls the door shut, leaving me alone.

"Rev. You didn't…you didn't make this up did you? You're not giving this statement to the police to help get your boyfriend off the hook?" Evan asks.

Wow. I can't believe he just said that. "Are you serious right now with that question?"

"Come on, I had to ask. It's just…it's so unlike you to go from being the goody goody little sister, always wanting to be perfect at the beginning of summer, to end up messing around with the help by the end of the summer and spending the night at his place alone. You have to realize how this looks," he says. "You went totally against character."

I'm sure everything I've done since the summer looks completely out of character but I don't really care what anyone thinks, even Evan. And his opinion has become the one that matters the most. "I would never lie about something like this, Evan. I swear. I'm telling the truth. Nick was with me that night. He never left my side." He barely left the bed the entire night.

"I just wanted to make sure. Didn't want you caught up in something that was bigger than the both of you."

"Like Mom and Dad," I murmur.

"Yeah. Exactly. They bit off way more than they could chew," Evan says. "I'm not calling you a liar or anything I just know…it's easy to get caught up in stuff. Look at our parents. I bet they didn't start off intending to steal from the parishioners."

We've never really talked about what our parents did. Never so bluntly, at least. "I'm sure they didn't."

"Right. We all try our best at life. Sometimes we end up doing something wrong and there's no going back."

"Are you implying Nick might've done something wrong?"

"I think that dude has bad luck. There's no other explanation for all the shit that's happened to him."

Maybe I could be Nick's good luck charm. He needs one.

And I want to be that for him. I want to be everything for him.

Chapter
TWENTY-TWO

8 p.m.

I'm scrolling through my phone when Reverie slips back into my bedroom, looking cute as hell wearing one of my T-shirts and nothing else. The shirt is big on me and it positively dwarfs her, hitting her just about mid-thigh and offering me a sweet glimpse of those long, pretty legs.

Glancing up from my phone, I watch her, entranced with the way she moves, the smile on her face, her long, wavy hair a tangled mess about her head. She looks gorgeous. Happy.

She looks like she belongs to me.

"Whatcha doing?" she asks as she crawls into bed beside me, snuggling close and resting her chin on my shoulder as I continue to look at my phone.

"Checking out stuff." I pause to look at her. "So. Is Evan mad at you?"

"More like he's worried," she answers. "He wanted to know if I'm at the bus station yet."

"Yeah, about that. I don't know if you'll be able to make it out tonight." I go to my local news station's app, bringing it up to the main page. It's full of reports on the weather and the havoc the storm has wrecked, especially over the last few hours. "There are floods everywhere in the area causing road blockages. Fallen trees bringing with them power lines so the electricity is out in the more rural parts. And there are some major accidents snarling up traffic on the highways. It doesn't look good. I don't know if I want you out there."

I love his protective streak. It makes me feel cherished. "Then I'll just stay here with you." She tilts her head to the side, her cheek pressed to my bare shoulder before she turns her head and drops a kiss on my skin. She makes it sound so easy, but I know her brother would absolutely shit if she weren't on that bus in the next hour. "I don't want to leave tonight anyway. I'd rather stay here with you."

I'd rather she stayed with me too but I need to respect her brother's wishes. I don't need that guy pissed at me. "We should at least try to go to the bus station and see what's going on, don't you think?"

She pulls away from me so we can look at each other fully. "Can't we just call and check on the schedule? I really don't want to go down there if I can't leave tonight."

"Good idea. I'll call now." I go into the web browser and look up the local bus station, pushing the link for the number so my phone makes the call. I let it ring for ten rings. Fifteen. I lose count after a while and finally hang up. "No answer. I'm guessing it must be busy."

A heavy sigh leaves her. "I don't want to go down there if it's crazy." She leans her head toward the window. The storm still rages on, we can both hear it in the otherwise stillness of the room. The gust of wind against my window is harsh, bringing with it a hard smattering of raindrops hitting the glass. "It still sounds awful out there."

"Yeah." I'm torn. I want to do what her brother wants me to but I also want to be selfish and keep her with me for the night. I know Evan would want us to be safe… he would never forgive me if something happened to his sister on my watch. I wouldn't be able to forgive myself either. "You want to stay?"

"Yes. Yes, yes." She grins as she tosses her arms around my neck and presses a kiss to my cheek. I don't know if I've ever seen her look so happy. "Thank you, thank you."

I sling my arm around her waist and pull her into my lap so she's lying on her back, her head cradled by my thigh as she stares up at me. "You need to text Evan and tell him what's going on."

She nods solemnly, her smile still tickling the corners of her mouth. "I will. I swear."

"Tell him we did it for safety reasons. And I'll have you on the bus back home tomorrow," I continue. I want to make this right with Evan, not have him believe we're defying him on purpose.

Though maybe we are. Just a little bit.

Reverie mock pouts. "I don't want to go home."

"Yes, you do. This place gives you the creeps, remember?"

"Not when I'm with you," she says.

Ah, this girl. She's going to make it impossible for me to be away from her for even a minute. "We're going to make this work, huh?"

Her pout fades, replaced with a look of concern. "We'll make what work? Us?"

I nod, unable to put into words how I feel about her. What we shared earlier had been so...monumental. I've had sex with girls but never was the act as meaningful as it is when I'm with Reverie.

Sounds like I'm quoting a cheesy romantic movie, but it's true. I don't want this girl to leave my side. I know I should let her go and live her life without me holding her back but what just happened has ruined all of my good intentions.

Now I just want to be selfish. And by being selfish that means I'm claiming Reverie as mine. She belongs to me.

Only me.

"We can totally make this work," she says with complete and utter sincerity. "I'll graduate high school in a few months and then we can do whatever we want."

"Yeah? What do you want to do?" I ask, bending over her with a sly grin.

She wraps her hand around the back of my neck, pulling me down for her kiss. "There are lots of things I want to do with you," she murmurs against my lips.

"I'm sure." I reach out and tickle her, just beneath the ribs, and she starts squirming in my arms, shouting her laughter and slapping at me, urging me to stop. But I don't. I keep tickling her until we're both in a tangle of arms and legs, our mouths fused, our bodies eventually becoming fused as we come together.

Yeah. I don't want this to end. We can make this work.

We have to.

I'm dreaming someone is pounding a hammer into a wall, the

sound so rhythmic that when it stops, my eyes pop open. I stare up at the ceiling, Reverie's head resting on my shoulder as she sleeps, her hair streaming all over my chest, stray strands tickling my face. I purse my lips and blow it away, freezing when I hear the pounding start up again.

I wasn't dreaming about that sound. Someone is knocking on my door in the middle of the damn night.

Sliding out of the bed as quietly as I can so I don't disturb Reverie, I go to the front door, looking through the peephole to see who's on the other side. But it's so dark outside, I can't tell.

"I know you're in there. Open the door, asshole!"

Shit. It's Hal Benson.

I crack open the door and peek through it. "I don't want any problems and I don't think you do either so if I were you I'd walk away before I call the cops."

Hal laughs, staggering on my doorstep. He tips sideways, and in a flash of a second I think he's going to collapse but he reaches out, slapping his hand against the wall so he can brace himself. "That's rich, you calling the cops. Go for it. I dare you."

Jackass has my number. No way do I want to draw their attention back to me, especially with Krista's dad involved. Frustrated, I grip the door handle, gritting my teeth as I ask, "What do you want?"

"I want you to tell me the truth. Man to man." His expression goes somber and he stands up straighter. "No one else is around. It's time to come clean, kid. Did you kill my daughter?"

I can almost feel sorry for him. Yeah, he's drunk. He wasn't the best father to Krista but he took care of her when she needed it. They were all each other had, kind of like how Mom and I were. Mom hated Hal Benson, thought he was a no good, angry drunk and she was right.

But he's a man in mourning, suffering through the terrible loss of his daughter. For that alone, I want to offer him sympathy.

"I'm sorry for your loss. I understand what it feels like since I just lost my mom a few months ago too," I say, irritated when I see the familiar nasty gleam light his eyes.

"You don't know shit," he mutters but I ignore him, just keep throwing the words out so he shuts up.

"I know you're hurting and I wish I could help you but I'm not the one who killed Krista. I would never do anything like that to hurt her. She was my friend."

"A friend you treated like shit the last few weeks of her life," Hal points out, dropping his hand from the wall, which only causes him to start weaving again.

The man is drunk as hell. He reeks of booze and sweat and his clothes are stained. Who knows when was the last time he bathed. The rain has lessened but it's still falling and it's bitterly cold outside. His hair is soaked and he doesn't have a coat on. He needs to go back home.

"You're right. We had our problems. We should've never dated but we did and that's what ruined our friendship. We argued a lot but nothing I would kill her over. You have to know that," I say, opening the door wider so I can really look at him. Let him see me. "You've known me a long time, Hal. Since I was a little kid. Have you ever seen a violent streak in me?"

"You went to jail once before," he points out. "For a violent crime."

"That I never committed," I point out. "They let me go. You know I wouldn't hurt Krista, Hal. You *know* it."

He slowly shakes his head, looking torn. Looking sad. "You were a good kid, Nicky. You always did right by your mama. I got thrown when they put you in jail and accused you of killing that guy. I've been thrown by that for years. I just…I don't know who else could've hurt my girl like that. That monster raped her. He strangled her with his bare hands. You know how hard that is? How long it takes? He must've stared straight into her eyes while choking the life out of her. How can someone do that?" Hal starts to cry, tears streaming down his face, dropping off his jaw. Despite his drunkenness of only a minute ago, he seems to have sobered up with the conversation.

"I'm sorry," I say with utter sincerity, horrified at the details he's giving me. It's awful, what happened to Krista. I have to agree with Hal—what sort of monster could do this?

"That boy David had me half convinced you murdered her. He was a big help at first, giving me the support and saying all the right things." Hal shakes his head, running his hand beneath his nose to catch the snot before he rubs it against the side of his black sweater. Disgusting. "I had no one else on my side, everyone thought I did it. But that kid's been helping me since the morning I learned what happened. Claims he loved Krista more than anyone else. I believe him."

Great. That Hal fell so easily for David's words irritates me. Everyone seems to believe what that guy says—except for me. "I'm glad he's been there for you," I practically choke out. "Maybe you should get back on home, Hal. It's late and it's cold out here."

"Yeah." He takes a step toward me, the overwhelming stench of alcohol and body odor blowing right at me, making me wrinkle my nose. "I've taken to wandering around the complex this time every night, hoping I'll find who killed her."

That's just sad. "I'm guessing whoever did it is long gone."

"Fucker," Hal spits out, his anger directed at someone else, not me. Thank God. "I hope he rots in hell."

"He will. They'll catch him and he'll have to pay for what he did." I start to close the door but Hal snakes an arm out, halting my progress.

"You'd tell me if you knew anything, wouldn't you Nicky? You wouldn't hide anything from me, right?" His bloodshot gaze implores me and my heart tugs in answer. I may not like this man very much but I've known him since I can remember.

"I've been nothing but honest with you from the very beginning," I tell him solemnly.

Hal nods once and backs away. "I appreciate that. Thank you."

Without another word he turns and staggers away, heading back to his apartment. I watch until I can't see him any longer, my head and heart heavy. Krista's death is ruining him and it's a hard thing to witness. Not finding her killer is eating him up inside. He needs an answer and proper support. Not the kind that David is offering him either.

I don't trust him. No one should.

Sighing heavily, I shut and lock the door, turning to find Reverie standing in the middle of the living room, eyes wide, lips pursed and looking unsure. "How long have you been here?"

"Long enough to hear some of your conversation with Krista's father," she says as she starts to approach me. She's still clad in my T-shirt, her hair in a knot on top of her head, thick pink socks on her feet. "You were very nice to him."

I shrug, uncomfortable. "He's had a tough time."

"But he's treated you so terribly since she died," Reverie points out.

I told her all about our confrontation earlier at the police department, my conversation with David, how close I came to beating his ass. She offered her unconditional support as usual but she also warned me that I needed to watch out. I don't need to push too far and end up with real criminal charges brought against me.

"He's hurting. When I first opened the door he started yelling at me but after a while I think…I really think I got through to him. He knows in his heart I didn't kill Krista. He's just looking for someone to blame."

She stares at me so quietly for so long I start to get uncomfortable. Maybe I did the wrong thing. Is she mad at me for talking to Hal? I might've given him ammunition to use against me later, not that I said anything incriminating. You never know what's going to set people off.

"You have such a big heart," she finally says, her voice scratchy. She comes to me and wraps her arms around my waist, pressing her cheek against my chest. "You should've turned him away. Instead, you tried to make him feel better."

"I've known him since I was a kid. He's not a great guy but he's still human." I rest my cheek against the top of her head, breathing in her sweet scent. "You're right. I do need to get out of here," I admit quietly.

She pulls away so quick she almost knocks against my chin. Her eyes wide, she stares up at me. "Are you serious?"

"Yeah. I can't stay here, Reverie. This place will suck me dry if I don't leave." I send her a stern look when she starts to open her mouth, cutting her off. "But I'm not coming to live with you or anything like that. Evan would shit."

She bursts out laughing. "He would not." Her laughter dies. "Well, maybe he would, but it doesn't matter. I want you to come and at least live by us. Evan could help you find a job and so could I. We have a few connections now. And maybe you could find your own apartment or get a roommate. Rent is a lot more expensive where I'm at."

Nerves buzz in my veins, settle in my gut. How am I ever going to afford this? I'm taking a chance here. Moving from the only town I've ever known to a new place, all for what? A girl?

For a girl and a chance at a new life. You're not really living if you're stuck here.

"You'll be fine." Reverie reaches out and cups my cheek, her fingers stroking lightly over my skin. "We'll help you. I want you there. I need you there, Nick."

I don't answer her, just pull her into my arms and hold her tight, overwhelmed with emotion for this girl, for this entire day. I've been on an emotional roller coaster from the moment we arrived in town and I'm ready to get back to normal.

If I even know what normal really is.

Chapter
TWENTY-THREE

November 15th

I sit on my knees on the couch that backs up against the front window and stare out at the parking lot, my gaze fixed on Nick's truck sitting nearby. I left my travel bag out there, the one I brought just in case something happened and I couldn't get back home. There's a change of clothes inside of it, my toiletries, a small makeup bag.

The rain has tapered down to a light but steady drizzle and the sky is still dark despite it being past eight in the morning. I woke up almost an hour ago, unable to fall back to sleep, hating the uneasiness that slipped over me after Krista's dad stopped by and spoke to Nick. I keep telling myself everything will be fine. Everything will work out the minute we get out of here.

But I'm not so sure. I have to go back home alone, on the bus. Nick has to take care of a few personal things first before he can even attempt to leave. He has to give notice on his apartment, quit his job, pack up his things. What if after I'm gone, he changes his mind? It could happen. Our idea is crazy. I know people will tell us we're too young to fall in love. Time will change everything and we'll eventually grow apart, blah, blah, blah.

Those were pretty much Evan's words to me and I get what he's saying, I really do. He's probably right. We *are* too young to get so serious so fast. But I'm not ready to give up on us now. I can't. Being away from Nick, even for a little bit...

Makes me nervous.

What else is making me nervous is running out to that parking lot and grabbing my bag. I cracked open the blinds only a few minutes ago, contemplating whether I should attempt going outside or not. Nick's keys rest on the kitchen counter. It would be easy enough to grab them, go out to his truck and unlock his door so I can grab my stuff. He's still asleep, I can hear him breathing deeply all the way in the living room and I don't want to disturb him.

It was so hard leaving the bed too. He's so warm and cozy and with us locked away in his bedroom, no one disturbing us, it feels like we're in our own little world. He wouldn't wake up and I didn't want to disturb him since he seemed so tired, falling into such a deep sleep he hardly moved.

Eventually, I got too antsy laying there, my mind filled with possibilities, many of them unpleasant. I finally crawled out of bed, unable to take it any longer. And now I'm dying to take a shower. I need to get ready so we can leave for the bus station. Evan has already texted me twice, asking what's going on, and I gave him noncommittal answers both times because really, I have no idea what's happening.

All I know is that I have to leave Nick. And I don't want to.

A woman appears in the parking lot, accompanied by two little girls who look a lot like her. She's holding their hands as she leads them to her car that's parked pretty close to Nick's. Her daughters are wearing bright pink puffy jackets, the color vivid against the otherwise gray morning, and seeing them out there, acting so normal, like it's any other day, spurs me on.

Leaping up, I grab Nick's keys and go to the door, unlocking it with a quick twist of my wrist. I'm already dressed and ready to go since I'm wearing yesterday's clothes and shoes. When I emerge outside, I drag in a sharp breath, startled by the crisp cold in the air. I scurry over to Nick's truck, looking around me, aware of my surroundings at all times just like my brother taught me.

I climb into the truck and reach behind the passenger seat, snagging the handle of my small bag. Breathing deep, I stay like that for a minute, my knees on the seat, my head bent as I inhale Nick's scent that still lingers. The woman with her cute girls drives by at the precise moment I finally back out of the truck and shut the door, offering me a friendly wave and I return it, seeing her making my pumping heart ease.

I'm safe. There's nothing to worry about.

Eager to get back to Nick so I can snuggle with him in bed for a few stolen minutes before I drag my butt into the bathroom and take a shower, I start toward his door, my steps faltering when a guy about my age appears out of nowhere, right in my path.

"Hey," he greets, his voice easy. Friendly. His entire demeanor is nonthreatening what with that pleasant smile on his face, the hood of his black North Face black fleece jacket pulled over his head, his hands in his jeans' pockets. He acts like he knows me and I wonder for a moment if we've ever encountered each other before.

"Hi." I come to a stop, my bag slung over my shoulder.

"You lost?"

I shake my head, frowning. "No. Do I look lost?"

"Oh. Sorry." He laughs. "I've just never seen you before. And I know everyone that lives here."

"Do you live here?"

"Well, yeah." He laughs again and shakes his head, as if my question was super lame. "Crazy storm yesterday, huh? You doing all right?"

Why would he ask if I'm doing all right? "I'm fine. And that storm was definitely crazy," I agree, starting to step around him as I lift my arm in a little wave. "See you around."

Before I can make my way toward Nick's front door the guy reaches out, his fingers curling around my upper arm and stopping me from leaving. I turn to look at him, slowly disengaging my arm from his gentle grip, wondering what the heck he wants.

"Are you visiting someone?" he asks, his voice low and dark.

Okay. This guy is being sort of creepy. "How is that any of your business? What are you, the plain clothes security guy who prowls the lot?" I'm sort of joking, sort of not. I don't like how this guy is acting.

His smile and nonthreatening stance evaporate in an instant. He's scowling, his hands going to his hips. "When there are strangers loitering around the complex, I make it my business."

"I'm not loitering." I lift my chin, tilting my head toward the building where Nick's apartment is. "You're right. I'm visiting someone."

"Who?"

I start to walk again, uncomfortable with this guy's constant questions. "See you later."

"Hey." He barks the word out, coming after me to grab hold of my arm and yank me around, his grip tight, his fingers biting into my skin even through the thick fabric of my sweatshirt. "You can't just walk away from me like that."

"Let go of me." I struggle against his hold, panic rising within me. If I screamed loud enough, would Nick hear? Would anyone hear? Is this how Krista felt when she encountered the person who eventually killed her? I'm being completely irrational but this guy is scaring me. "What's your problem?"

"*You're* my problem." He pulls me close into him, thrusting his face in mine. His dark, angry eyes stare straight into me and I shrink within his grasp, frightened by what I see—which is absolutely nothing. His eyes are flat. Dead. "You and your stupid boyfriend."

"I-I don't know what you're talking about." Who is this guy? What does he want from me? I shouldn't have come out here, lulled by the supposed safety I saw in the normalcy of the woman walking with her children. I should've woken Nick up and asked him to come with me. How could I have been so stupid? He would've come with me. He probably would've run out here and grabbed the bag and made me wait inside. He'd do anything for me.

But can he save me now?

"You know exactly what I'm talking about." He pauses, the gleam in his eyes growing, the light against the dark vivid. Scary. "Reverie."

Chapter
TWENTY-FOUR

I wake up to my bed empty, the space Reverie occupied next to me long gone cold. Sitting up, I run my hands through my hair and look around, my vision blurry, my head fuzzy. Didn't get much sleep last night.

Not that I mind. I was occupied with...other things.

Namely Reverie.

Heaving a deep breath, I reach over to my bedside table and grab my cell, checking my text messages. I don't have many, which is normal. There are two from Evan, who I gave my number to before I left with Reverie. He's asking both times when are we leaving for the bus station and I send him a quick reply, saying we should be there within the hour.

I'll take a quick shower, we'll grab breakfast on the way, and I'll put Reverie on that damn bus myself if I can. I don't want her to leave but she has to get back to school and work. And I need to put together a quick plan to get myself out of here.

Feeling good, I climb out of bed and go into the bathroom to take care of business. None of the towels are damp and I figure Reverie wants to take a shower before we leave so it's on my mind to tell her exactly that when I emerge into the living room.

But she's not there.

She's not in the kitchen either. There are not many other places she can be in my apartment but I look around anyway, as if she's hiding from me in some dark corner, ready to yell out 'surprise!' when I discover her.

Panic rises within me as I hear nothing but eerie silence. She's not in my apartment. I throw open the front door and barge right outside in just my sweats and nothing else, my feet still bare, my chest exposed to the cold air and rain. My truck is still there, right where I left it and the parking lot is mostly quiet.

A bag sits in the middle of the walkway, close to my front door. It's black with a floral print. I remember Reverie bringing something very similar with her when we left her place, a change of clothes she wanted to have just in case something happened and she had to stay with me.

We got our wish. But where is she now?

I approach the bag and pick it up, zipping it open so I can look at the contents inside. The clothes look like something she would wear. I'm fairly certain it's her fucking bag.

What the hell does this mean? Where did she go?

Glancing around I see nothing unusual, no one around. I immediately call Evan, waiting impatiently for him to answer.

"Have you heard from Reverie?" I ask the moment I hear his voice.

He doesn't sound that thrilled to hear from me. "She texted me about twenty minutes ago and said you two were on your way to the bus station. Why? Have you left yet?"

"No." I start jogging back to my apartment, her bag still clutched in my other hand. "I just woke up.'"

"Well, where the hell is she? You two need to get going, it's nearly ten."

"I…" I close my eyes, unsure how to say this. He's going to fucking kill me. "I don't know where she is."

"What the fuck are you talking about?" Evan's voice blasts at me through the phone so loud I have to hold it away from my ear. "How could you lose my sister you asshole? Where is she?"

"Fuck, I don't know okay? I'm gonna go look for her right now. I'm sure it's nothing. I'll call you right back."

"It better be nothing dickwad. You better find my sister." Evan's on a roll when I hang up on him, cursing me out but I can't blame him.

Shit. Shit, shit, shit. I don't know where she is. I don't know where she could've gone. I text her, sending her a quick *where are you* but she doesn't reply and I'm starting to panic.

Fine. I'm in full-on panic mode because I don't know where the hell she's at. I gotta find her. If something happened to her, I could never forgive myself.

She doesn't reply to my texts and I head for Hal Benson's apartment, rapping on his door with such force the wood rattles on its hinges with my knock. He might've seen something. Hell, I doubt it but I need to ask.

"What the fuck you knocking like that for, son?" Hal asks the moment he swings open the door. "You 'bout scared me to death."

He looks awful, like he just crawled out of bed, wearing a stained white T-shirt and faded blue and white striped pajama pants. His hair is sticking straight up and he scratches at his belly.

"Sorry. Didn't mean to wake you. I'm uh, looking for my friend. She's about this tall." I hold up my hand at just below my shoulder. "With blond hair and blue eyes. Really pretty."

"Aren't they all really pretty, the girls you hang out with?' Hal cackles and I push down the frustration that rises within me. I don't have time for these games.

"Have you seen her?" I ask again. "I think she's...lost." I make her sound like a missing pet but damn it, I don't know what could've happened to her. When did she wake up? How long has she been gone?

I have no idea.

"Nope. Haven't seen any pretty blondes wandering around here lost and alone. Tell her when you find her that's dangerous in this area. I hope you find her soon." He slams the door in my face before I get a chance to say anything else and I'm left standing there, unsure of what to do next. I don't want to call the cops because they're nothing but trouble but who else can give me the help I need? Hal is hungover so not like I'm going to ask him. He's useless. I've got no one in this godforsaken town except for Reverie and now I've fucking lost her too.

Where in the hell *is* she?

"Hey bro, what are you doing here?"

I turn to find David striding toward me, the same shitty smile he wore yesterday still on his face. He is the last person I want to see. "I could ask you the same question," I mutter.

"I'm just checking in on Hal, like usual. Poor guy needs me, especially on Sunday mornings. He tends to binge drink on Saturdays for some reason. I guess it's because he's off work and has nothing to occupy his mind." The smile on his face never fades. It's like he has it glued on. "Were you just in there with him? How's he doing?"

"I spoke to him for a little bit. He's fine. A little hungover but he'll survive." I run a hand over my chin, a shiver stealing over my skin at the pointed way David watches me.

"What happened to you anyway? You're definitely not dressed for this kind of weather." David's gaze is bright as he looks at me, slowly shaking his head. "I'd guess you just ran out of your apartment. You don't even have shoes on. What's the rush?"

"I'm um, looking for someone."

David frowns, his expression one of perfect concern. "Who you looking for?"

"My friend." I pause. I don't want to give this guy any details but I'm desperate. He could help me. "Reverie."

"Ah, the infamous Reverie." David nods, as if he's just ran into her and knows exactly where she is. We're wasting precious time chatting like it's no big thing when I need to find her. "Haven't seen her."

"Are you sure? Do you even know what she looks like?"

"Blond, cute and pure as the driven snow? Nope, I am positive I haven't seen her around. But I just got here so…" He shrugs.

"Okay, thanks. I need to go." I start to leave but David calls my name and I turn to face him, jogging backwards. I need to get dressed and make phone calls. I don't have time to talk to this asshole. "What?"

"Hope you find her soon." David grins but his eyes are black. Dead. Uneasiness slips down my spine like ice, making me shiver. "Wouldn't want anything bad to happen to her." The dark chuckle that follows is bone chilling.

And that's when it hits me. He knows. This motherfucker knows where she is.

Everything inside of me goes cold and I start for him but he's faster. He dodges into Hal's apartment, slamming the door shut and turning the lock with such force I hear the bolt slide into place. I bash my fist against the door, the thin wood seeming to give with my every punch as I command David to open it.

"Open up, God damn it!" I yell, kicking at the door now, smashing my toes since I'm not wearing shoes. Not the smartest move to make but fuck it. It's like I can't even feel anything, I'm pumped so full of adrenaline and fear. "Tell me where she is!"

David says nothing but I know he's in there, which only infuriates me more. I'm pulling out my phone, ready to call the cops and then

Evan when the door swings open, Hal standing in the doorway. I have a total moment of déjà vu. Didn't we just go through this not ten minutes ago? "What's your problem, son?"

"You're a liar, that's my problem." I push my way inside, calling Reverie's name as I make my way through the small apartment, looking in every room. The place is a disaster, clutter and trash everywhere, empty liquor bottles rolling on the floor. I kick past them, peeking in the bathroom, in Hal's room, my hand going for the knob that I know will open Krista's room when Hal screams at me, making me pause.

"Don't you dare go in my baby's room," Hal says, his voice ragged. "Stay out of there. No one's allowed inside."

"Where's David? Do you let him go in there?" My breathing is harsh, my ears roaring with the sound, my heart pounding so hard it feels like it's going to burst out of my chest. "Tell me."

"I told you. I don't let anyone in Krista's room."

"So where is he?" I don't know if I believe him. I can sense someone is behind that door. I don't know if it's David or Reverie or the both of them but I want inside that damn room. I have to see it for myself to prove it's empty.

"He flew out of the sliding glass door not two minutes ago." Hal indicates with his hand before he scratches the back of his head. "What are you boys fighting about now?"

"He took my girl." I go for the slider and pull it open, walking outside. The yard is small and nothing but mud. And I'm the only one standing on the tiny crumbling cement slab substituting as a patio. David is long gone. I turn to find Hal standing in the open doorway, watching me with bleary eyes. "I need your help, Hal. I need to find Reverie."

"Reverie? What the hell kind of name is that?" Hal keeps his gaze fixed on me as I walk back into his apartment and shut the sliding glass door. My gaze locks on the door to Krista's room and the urge to go inside is so strong I can hardly stand it.

"When was the last time you went in Krista's room?" I ask, making my way there.

"Why, I never go in there. Once, right after she died, I sat on her bed and cried like a baby for hours. It's sacred ground to me. Too hard for me to go in there right now, it's just too soon. I can't take it, seeing her stuff, smelling her smell." Hal sniffs and wipes at his eyes.

Jesus. I'm going to feel like an asshole if I'm wrong but something is telling me my instincts are spot on. "I need to go in there. I won't disturb anything but let me at least look, okay? I need to check on something."

"There's nothing to check. My Krista is gone." Hal is full blown crying now, collapsing into a rickety dining chair nearby, the wood creaking from his weight. "I don't want you in there, Nick. You have no right to be in my baby's room."

I defy him. There is just no way I'm not looking in that room. I turn the doorknob, frustrated when I find it's locked and I slam my shoulder against the wood, again and again.

I'm getting in that room. I'll feel like a dumbass if I'm wrong but... I don't think I'm wrong.

"Stop!" Hal cries, rushing toward me. He grabs at my shoulders but I'm stronger than him and I shrug him off, hitting the door again, my shoulder aching, my arm throbbing. The wood starts to splinter, encouraging me to keep going and I barge into the door at full force, triumph surging inside of me when the frame cracks and the door swings open.

Reverie's sitting on her knees in the center of Krista's bed, her arms bound behind her back, duct tape covering her mouth. Her eyes are wide above the strip of metallic gray tape, and I can hear her muffled screams. I rush toward her, my heart stalled in my chest, seeing her like this. "Baby," I whisper, reaching for her.

"Not so fast." A hand snags around the waistband of my sweatpants, pulling me backward and right into fucking David himself. He must've been standing on the other side of the door, just waiting for me to bust it open. "Look at you, running in here like the hero you should've been for Krista."

I turn to glare at him, my heart falling to my gut when I see he has a knife in his hand, the light from above glinting off the steel of the blade, showing off just how sharp it is. "Let her go. This isn't about her. It's about you and me," I tell him after taking a deep breath, trying to keep my voice calm. I don't want to agitate him more. He could hurt her.

Or me.

"No way am I letting her go. She's as perfect as a picture, sitting there bound and gagged, driving you crazy. It drives you crazy, right? Seeing her like that?" I say nothing and he scowls, pissed that he didn't get a reaction I'm sure. "You took something from me so I'm going to take something from you. Only fair, I say." He smiles and lifts the blade so he can stare at his reflection. "Your silly virgin is dumber than I thought. It was so easy, grabbing her."

I remain silent, sliding Reverie a quick look. She's struggling against the ties that bind her wrists, tears streaming down her cheeks. My heart breaks just looking at her. I didn't protect her. I wasn't there to save her from this maniac just like I didn't save Krista either.

"I should take that back, calling her a virgin. She's nothing but a little slut now that you've fucked her a few times." David makes a tsking noise and shakes his head. "Shame it's going to have to end so soon."

My blood is boiling and I swear my head is about to explode. I can't stand what he's saying about Reverie but I refuse to react. That's exactly what he's looking for.

"Don't have anything to say? Interesting. Well, if you must know, after everything that happened with Krista, I knew I had to do something to get back at you. That entire night didn't go as planned and I regret so much what happened. It's all your fault you know, that she's gone."

"Who?" I squint at him, noticing how frantic he appears. He's looking all around the room, at Krista's belongings, taking note of all of it. It's almost like she's still alive, what with her clothes still strewn everywhere, a bunch of makeup littered on the top of her dresser, along with various perfume bottles and hair stuff. Posters on the wall and photos of her and her friends stuck to the mirror.

Even a picture of the three of us; me, Krista and David, our arms around each other with Krista standing in between us, most likely taken before David and I were first thrown in jail.

A lifetime ago.

"Krista!" Her name explodes from his lips, making me flinch, and he starts to pace the room, running his fingers over everything he can touch. "I haven't been in here since that night. When I came to see her."

My entire body goes still. "You saw her that night?"

"I was with her the entire night." He throws his hands up into the air, a smile curling his lips for the briefest moment. "Almost had her convinced she didn't need you either. She was so damn stuck on you. Always had been. I'm the one she used. She would actually say that to my face, like some sort of heartless bitch. That made me so mad and she knew it. You're the one she really wanted and I gotta admit, that drove me fucking crazy, Fairfield. I wanted to be the one she needed and I told her that but she wouldn't listen."

"What did you do, David?" I don't know if I want to know, if I want to hear this. But I have to. For me. For Hal. For Reverie.

"I fucked her, right where your little girlfriend is tied up, right in the middle of her squeaky bed. We went at it for hours since Hal was gone, out drinking like usual. I worked hard to please her that night. So damn hard. I wanted to erase you from her memory once and for all but she just smiled and said she loved me like a friend after it was all over. That killed me." David hangs his head for a moment, staring at the knife as he turns it this way and that in his hands.

I look at Reverie again, trying to tell her with my eyes, my expression, that everything's going to be all right. I'll get her out of this. She stares back at me, her chest heaving, the tears still coming down her face, and my heart is fucking ready to burst wide open from the pain seeing her like this causes me.

"After we were done Krista got dressed and did her hair. Redid her makeup. Said she wanted to look pretty just for you. Only for you. I just had sex with her and she was going to you." David lifts his head, his eyes as black as night, his skin pale. He looks terrible. Scary. "I lost it. Just fucking…lost it. Like a baby I crawled out of bed and begged her not to go. Told her I loved her, said I would do anything for her but she wouldn't listen. She just wanted to get to you."

"I never saw Krista that night, David," I say as a reminder, though I'm pretty damn certain I know what he's going to say next.

The horror that threatens to consume me is strong. Overwhelming. I need to get Reverie away from him before he does something to her too.

"I know. I never let her leave this room." He smiles, as if lost in a fond memory. "I tried to block the door so she couldn't leave to go see you but she shoved me out of the way and I fell to the floor. Didn't know little Krista was so strong."

Nausea threatens and I think I'm going to be sick.

"Before she could open the door I lunged for her and tackled her to the ground. She was so soft beneath me, her skirt riding up her thighs as she kicked at me with those sexy high heels she loves to wear. I pinned her down, wrapped my hands around her wrists and pressed them to the floor. She struggled so much, calling me all sorts of names, demanding that I let her go. But I didn't. I kissed her instead and that's when things got ugly." David pauses, imploring me with a look. "She slapped me. Can you believe it? The bitch actually slapped my face as hard as she could. I got so mad I backhanded her, marking her face too. And she just laughed at me."

Jesus. I don't want to hear anymore but I don't want to stop him either. I'm a witness to his confession and so is Reverie. David killed Krista. He killed her right here in her own bedroom and then went on to become Hal's biggest support while they looked in vain for information to find Krista's killer. When he was the guilty one all along.

What sort of sick fuck does this?

"She made me so mad I told her to stop laughing but she wouldn't. She just kept doing it. Calling me a pussy. Calling me all sorts of names. I couldn't take it. She always treated me that way and I couldn't take it anymore so I told her to shut up. And when she wouldn't shut up I put my hands around her skinny little neck and squeezed. Her eyes bulged out of her head and she slapped at my hands, trying to make me stop but I wouldn't stop. I couldn't stop. I had to shut her up once and for all and once I realized she wasn't moving anymore, I started to cry."

I edge closer to the bed, closer to Reverie so I can grab her and keep her safe with me. This entire story is freaking me out. If David could do that to Krista, someone he supposedly loved, then what could he do to me or Reverie?

"So it was an accident," I say softly, not wanting to startle him, but my words seem to snap him out of the trance telling the story put him in.

"What are you doing over there? Get away from her!" David waves his hand around, the knife slicing the air. "And *of course*, it was an accident. I never meant to kill Krista. And you're the one who pushed me to do it. If she didn't love you so damn much, everything would've been fine between us. Just fine. You ruined *everything.*"

I don't say anything because I'm not about to argue with crazy. He can go ahead and put the blame on me. "What happened next?"

"I cried and cried and slapped at her face, trying to wake her up but she was gone. Gone, gone, laying right there, in front of her door." He points at the ground not far from where he's standing. "I picked her up and brought her to the bed and stroked her hair. Made love to her one last time."

Details I did not want to know.

"And then I wrapped her in an old blanket I found in her closet and took her with me. I was going to take her away but I got scared. Heard people walking around so I dumped her close to her door outside and just…left. No one saw me." He tilts his head back and starts to weep. "I hate what happened. I hate that we lost her. It's so unfair, what she did to me. All I ever wanted to do was love her."

"I'm sure she did love you." I come closer to the bed and reach out, resting my hand on Reverie's knee. I can feel her trembling beneath my palm and all I want is to console her.

"Fuck you. She did not. Not the way she loved you." He strides toward the bed, the knife pointed straight at me. I drop my hand from Reverie's knee and he notices, thrusting the knife toward where she sits. "I should take her away from you. See how that makes you feel."

"Leave her out of this." Fear clouds my head and I shake it, jerking my thumb at my chest. "This is about me and you know it."

David's face crumples, his eyes squeezing out a few tears. They seem false but maybe that's because he just confessed he murdered Krista. "You stole everything from me, man. From the time we were little, you were always better than me at everything. I adored you and hated you all at once. I always loved Krista but when you two started going out, I was devastated. I had to win her back—and I did. But then I lost her. I lost her forever."

"You son of a bitch." The low snarl of Hal's voice fills the room, sending a chill down my spine and we both turn to find him filling the doorway, his expression incredulous. Wounded, like an injured animal.

An injured animal who is mean and ready to strike at those who come near.

"You killed my girl," Hal says, his gaze never leaving David. "All this time, pretending to be there for me and letting me cry on your shoulder while you vowed to do something and you're the one who murdered my baby."

"It's his fault!" David points at me at the same time he throws himself on the bed, grabbing hold of Reverie and pulling her so her back is to his front, the knife at her throat. "Don't come another step or I'll kill her too."

"Haven't you had enough with killing and destroying? What the hell is wrong with you? You've been wrecking lives for about as long as I've known you." Hal says, walking further into the room. He glances around, taking in all of his daughter's stuff before he squeezes his eyes shut tight, shaking his head. I notice then that he has a handgun dangling from his fingers.

Shit.

Chapter
TWENTY-FIVE

10:30 a.m.

My vision is blurry from all the tears I've shed and my face hurts from the tug of the duct tape on my skin. I feel like I can't breathe and I close my eyes, my chest tight from the sob I'm withholding.

David's arm is wrapped tight around my middle, the giant knife he's holding pressed at my throat. I'm frozen in his terrifying embrace, too scared to move though my entire body is trembling with fear. He's going to cut me. I know it. And once he starts, he might never stop.

"Let her go," Nick says, his voice even, his gaze full of fear. I stare at him, wishing I could speak, wishing he could read my mind.

I love you.

I'm sorry.

I should've never left you.

I screwed up.

Please forgive me.

"Why? So you can have everything yet again?" He drags the tip of the knife down the length of my neck, I can feel how sharp it is and I swear the blade pricks my skin. "You can't have her. This one's mine."

"Do as he says." Krista's dad lifts his right arm, the gun aimed right at David. Hal's arm is shaking, the gun wobbling this way and that and

I close my eyes, terrified he's going to accidentally shoot me. "Don't hurt another defenseless girl, David. Let that one go before you kill her too."

David laughs, the sound manic. "Defenseless. That's a good one. Krista was far from defenseless. She was the toughest damn girl I ever knew. She put up a fight till the very end."

If he thinks that's going to reassure her father, he has another thing coming. I wince, ready for the blow and I'm not disappointed.

"Shut the fuck up about my girl!" Hal roars. "You didn't know her!"

"I knew her better than you, old man. She hated you." David sneers as he presses the knife closer to my throat. This time I do feel the cut, the slice in my skin and I scream beneath the duct tape, the sound muffled but roaring in my ears.

Nick goes white as a sheet but otherwise doesn't react at all. "Jesus, David, you're going to slice her neck open. Let her the fuck go!"

David turns his head toward mine, his eyes staring at me, dark and fathomless. A gruesome smile curls his lips. "You're so pretty. No wonder Nick wants to protect you."

I close my eyes but he shakes me, making my head bobble. "Look at me!" My eyes pop open and his smile grows. "That's it. So pretty. So clean and sweet and perfect. Did you let him touch you? Of course, you did. Spent the night at his place again, huh? You're nothing but a filthy whore now, just like Krista."

"Shut your damn mouth!" Hal yells, taking a step toward the bed. I turn to see the gun pointed straight at us, his arm still shaking, his finger slipping over the trigger. I close my eyes again, not prepared to watch my death come right at me.

And that's when everything happens in a white-hot blur.

Nick leaps onto the bed, covering both David and me as his hand goes for David's wrist, squeezing so tight I hear the knife clatter to the floor. At the same moment the gun goes off, once. Twice. The sound deafening yet I can still hear the wiz of the bullet as it flies straight past my ear. A muffled groan sounds and I jerk against both boys who are holding me down, unable to tell who is who.

We fall from the bed to the floor in a tangle and I can hear Hal sobbing above us, murmuring words I can't understand. He runs off, where I don't know, and then I'm rolling away from the both of them, lying on the floor on my side with my back to them, trying to catch my breath and calm my racing heart.

Hands touch me, fingers traveling over my face before I hear a muttered 'sorry' and the tape is ripped from my mouth. A gasp escapes me, the pain excruciating as it tears at my skin, and I take in a great big gulp of air, my lungs burning from the intensity.

"You okay?" I turn to find Nick staring at me, his skin pale and little beads of sweat on his forehead. "I need to untie you."

I drink him in, happiness filling me, and I struggle to try and sit up. But it's hard with my hands tied behind my back. "Where is he?" I croak, my throat raspy from my screams.

"David? He's been hit," Nick says grimly, indicating with a flick of his head behind him. "He's not moving. Hal shot him."

"Oh, my God," I whisper, shock coursing through me. Nick reaches around my body, his fingers fumbling with the knot at my wrists, and I turn my back more toward him, keeping my eyes averted from where David lies. I can see his feet, his legs, but I don't want to see his face. What if Hal shot him there? What if he's dead?

"I'm gonna get you free," he says between gritted teeth. "Just give me…a…moment."

Frowning, I wait, twisting my wrists this way and that to assist him. Nick doesn't sound right. His breathing is shallow and his voice raspy. As if he's in pain. He presses against me as he undoes the last of the knot and his bare skin is cool to the touch.

When the knot is undone and I'm free again, I back away from him, gasping when I see the slow trickle of blood sliding from the bullet hole that mars his left shoulder. "Nick, you've been shot." I rear up on my knees and take the scarf that David used to bind my wrists and wrap it around Nick's upper arm. He winces and grunts when I touch him, his face going even paler if that's possible, and I pull him into my arms, hugging him close.

"You'll be fine," I whisper against his ear, looking around for Hal. Where is he? "We need to call the police, call an ambulance. We need to get you help." And David, I add silently. We can't just let him bleed out on Krista's bedroom floor. We don't even know the extent of his injuries.

"Just glad…you…didn't get…shot," Nick murmurs against my neck. He's leaning heavily against me and I'm trying my best to bear his weight but it's hard. He weighs a ton. "I tried my best…to save you."

"You did save me," I murmur, brushing my fingers through his hair, clutching him close. "I'm fine. And you'll be fine too. I promise."

"What about…him?" I feel Nick lift up and I know he's looking at David. "He hasn't moved, Reverie. Do you think he's dead?"

"I don't know. Don't worry about him. We need to concentrate on you." In the distance I can hear the faint wail of a siren and relief floods me, making me nearly lose my grip on Nick.

"He was my...best friend. All...three...of us were friends. I didn't know he felt like...that about...her."

"Stop talking." I shush him, murmuring silly words of comfort, yelling "in here!" when I hear the paramedics burst into Hal's apartment. They rush inside the bedroom, the police following right after them, asking to clear the scene for evidence, and then someone is picking me up by the shoulders, making me stand.

"I don't want to leave him," I say as I start to cry, my arms feeling empty, my heart aching. "Please."

"You can ride in the ambulance with him, honey," a female paramedic says, her voice full of sympathy as she wraps her arm around my shoulders and leads me away. "Come on, let's get you checked out before we load you up."

The paramedic leads me out of Krista's bedroom and I see the police are talking to Hal in the living room. He looks terrible, his expression full of remorse, his shoulders slumped. I wonder if the police will arrest him.

If David's dead, would they have to?

"Is the other boy okay?" I ask the paramedic once I'm seated in the back of the ambulance. "Is he going to live?"

The paramedic doesn't answer me for a while, just goes about her business of checking my vitals, her fingers probing the delicate skin of my wrist where I was bound before she checks the knife wound on my neck. "You're lucky that blade didn't penetrate your skin further," she murmurs as she applies antiseptic to the cut.

I meet her gaze and try to compose myself. "Please," I whisper. "Tell me what's going on."

She sighs and slowly shakes her head. "Your boyfriend is fine. The bullet seemed to go clean through his arm. They're bringing him into the ambulance right now. The other one...his injuries are more severe but I think he's going to make it."

"You do?" The relief that floods me is overwhelming. I know I shouldn't care if David lives or dies after everything he's done but I don't wish death on anyone. Even a boy who holds a knife to my throat and threatens to kill me.

"Yes," she says with a firm nod. "Now let's get you situated before they bring your boyfriend in. You can talk to him then, okay?"

"Is he conscious?"

"He's lucid, yes."

I wait for the stretcher to come into the ambulance and within minutes it appears, Nick lying on it, his eyes closed, his arm bandaged. I lean over him, pressing a kiss to his forehead, and he smiles.

The sight of that smile sends my heart racing to the sky.

"I look bad, huh?" he asks, his voice faint, that smile still curling his lips.

"You look tough." He looks beautiful. A little pale but alive, the bandage wrapped tight around his bare arm, his chest and stomach on display, his shoeless feet covered with mud. "I've never seen you look better."

"You're just saying that because you're glad I survived." He cracks open his eyes. "That scared the shit out of me."

"Me too," I admit.

"When he had that knife to your throat, I thought…" He shudders and closes his eyes. "I thought I was going to lose you."

I take the hand of his uninjured arm and lace our fingers together tight. I don't ever want to let him go. "I'm still here."

"Yeah." He swallows and winces. "Me too. My arm hurts like a son of a bitch."

"You're going to be fine. It'll be an awesome scar." I bring our linked hands up to my mouth and press a kiss to his knuckles.

"Hell yeah, it will." His eyes open again and he groans. "Your brother is going to kick my ass."

I laugh, the sound watery, and I realize I'm crying as well, the tears flowing down my cheeks and dropping onto his chest. "No, he won't. You saved my life."

"I did, didn't I?" His mouth curves into this little lopsided smile and it's the cutest thing I've ever seen. "You saved my life too, Rev. I don't know what I would do without you."

His words break down the walls I've held up for so long as I tried my best to be strong. I bend over Nick and cry, my face pressed against his chest, my tears dampening his skin. I can feel his heartbeat, his body solid and strong, and I cry harder at the thought of losing him.

But I didn't lose him. I won't ever let go of him again.

He squeezes my hand, his fingers so strong and sure that I know he'll be all right.

And so will we.

Chapter
TWENTY-SIX

Six months later

"Oh my God, you look gorgeous." I clasp my hands together to keep from reaching for him, my heart racing with pure pleasure at the sight of my boyfriend. "All the girls will be jealous of my prom date."

Nick glances down at himself, his mouth scrunched as he tugs at his bow tie, appearing uncomfortable and completely out of his element. "I'm doing this for you, I hope you realize this."

"I do. Trust me." I go to him and wrap my arms around his waist, kissing his smooth cheek. He smells delicious. "You look good in a tux."

"Yeah? Well, let me look at you." He reaches for my hands and pulls me away from him, his gaze drinking me in slowly, from the top of my head to the tips of my toes, his eyes getting wider and wider. "Hell, Rev. What are you wearing?"

"A question I need to ask as well," Evan says from behind me.

I turn to find my big brother scowling at me. I do a twirl, the skirt of my turquoise dress swirling around my legs. "You don't like it?"

"Too much skin showing. You should wear a sweater," he says, sounding like an old man. My brother, my protector. With the lawsuits and the possible jail time our parents are facing after what they did to

The Flock of the Lambs, they haven't called us in weeks. Maybe even a month. And when they do call, the conversations are all about them and how everyone has turned against them when they did no wrong.

They're completely delusional.

We're done with them, Evan and I. We're making it on our own. It wasn't our fault they stole. All sorts of reporters have tried to contact us to talk about what happened but we refuse to speak to them. Maybe someday, when it's not so painful to think about the way our parents first manipulated us, tricked us and then completely abandoned us.

For now, it's best we leave it alone and get on with our lives.

"A sweater?" I laugh and shake my head. "I don't think so."

"I love her dress. I think she looks beautiful," Nick says, his arm going around my waist, his hand splayed across the exposed skin of my back.

"I'm sure you do. Exactly for the reason I hate it." Evan shakes his head. "You two kids have fun at prom, okay?"

"Okay, Grandpa." I go to my brother and kiss his cheek, giving him a hug before I pull away from him. My lipstick left a smudge on his skin and I wipe it off with my fingertips, which makes him slap my hand away.

"Get out of here. Be back by midnight," he grumbles.

"Are you serious?" Nick and I got a hotel room for the night because you know...it's prom. And you're supposed to do that with your boyfriend on prom night.

"Nah, no curfew tonight." Evan points his finger at Nick. "But you keep her safe, you got that?"

"Always." Nick stands straighter, his back stiff. "I promise."

We drive to the auditorium where my senior prom is being held in the old truck, Nick griping about it almost the entire way there. But I wouldn't have it any other way. He wanted to spend money to rent a limo but I told him that was a waste. I didn't need anything else to make this prom night perfect.

Just him.

Normalcy. That's all I wanted since I first learned what my parents did and how their actions changed my life. I felt completely out of control. Lost. Deceived. But I finally have my life back, thanks to Evan and Nick and my friends—and it's even better than it was before. I was sheltered and silly and naïve. Now I feel strong. Smart. Like I can deal with anything.

After David abducted me and shoved me into Krista's room and the fight that ensued, things have changed dramatically. David is being held in jail without bail after recovering from his injuries at the hospital while under constant police and suicide watch. He's been charged with the murder of Krista Benson and the assault and kidnapping of me.

Hal Benson was never charged with the shooting of David or Nick. It was ruled as an act of self-defense in the case of David and accidental with Nick. Last we heard, Hal is in rehab, working hard toward his recovery.

Nick healed from his gunshot injury quick, thanks to the loving care of...me. Evan insisted he move in with us so we could take care of him while he was recovering and he's lived there ever since. Once I graduate school in less than three weeks, we're going to look into finding an apartment together in Santa Cruz, where I'll be going to college in the fall on a scholarship.

My future plans—which at one point seemed hopeless—all came together. How, I'm not quite sure, but I'm not going to question it.

I'm just so incredibly thankful I have Nick by my side.

We pull into the lot of my high school a few short minutes later, Nick parking the truck and turning off the engine. I watch some couples run past us, laughing and giggling, the boys wearing tuxedos, the girls in sparkly dresses. One of the girls waves at me and I smile and wave back, recognizing her from my English class. Once they're gone, I glance in Nick's direction to find him watching me.

"You look happy," he says, his low, warm voice sending a shiver down my spine.

My smile grows. "Because I am."

"Because you're going to prom?"

I swat him on the shoulder. "Because I'm with you."

He pulls me into him, kissing me until I can't breathe before he breaks away from me. "You look sexy as hell in that dress," he murmurs, his gaze roaming all over me, as if he can't figure out what to stare at first.

I raise my brows at him, every bit of my bare skin warming from the smoldering intensity in his eyes. "You like it?"

"I'll like it even more when I can take it off of you in our hotel room." My cheeks are instantly on fire and he laughs, shaking his head. "That I can still embarrass you is the cutest thing ever."

"Shut up," I say, feeling silly. Feeling happy. Content.

Loved.

"I have a gift for you." His voice and expression have gone solemn and I back away from him, surprised by this announcement.

"A gift?" I didn't get anything for him. Did we promise each other gifts?

"Yeah." He reaches into the front pocket of his tuxedo jacket and pulls out a tiny velvet jewelry box. "Open it."

I take it from him with trembling fingers, popping open the box. Inside is a thin white gold band, a tiny diamond in the center. I stare at it for a breathless second, shock and pleasure coursing through my veins, making my head swim. "What is this?" I ask, looking up at him.

He looks nervous. And cute. So cute. "A promise ring. I know it's not much but I wanted to let you know that I'm…I'm serious about this, Reverie. About us. When Evan tells me I have to protect you, I take that very seriously. And I want to protect you for as long as I can. Hopefully forever."

I can't take it when he says perfect things like that. Clutching the box in my hand, I throw myself at him, hugging him tight, a shiver moving through me when he circles his arms around my waist. "I love you," I whisper into his ear, my arms around his neck.

"I love you too." His arms tighten around me for a brief moment before he's pushing me away and reaching for the box still clutched in my hand. "Let me put it on your finger."

I hold out my trembling hand, giggling when he has trouble pulling the ring from its velvety confines. His hand is shaking too as he makes a few failed attempts before he finally slips the band on my ring finger.

It's a perfect fit.

"I love it," I breathe as I stare down at the ring on my finger. It's so dainty. So beautiful.

"It's too small."

Lifting my head, I glare at him. "It's perfect. I love it, almost as much as I love you."

"Good." He sounds relieved. How could he think I'd not love the ring and this special night? Everything about him and us together and the promise that he's made me? I've never been so happy. "Because I'm afraid you're stuck with me forever."

"I wouldn't have it any other way," I say as I lean in close for his kiss.

OWNING VIOLET

Coming December 2nd, 2014

New York Times **bestselling author Monica Murphy begins a sexy new contemporary romance series—perfect for fans of Christina Lauren and Emma Chase—that introduces three sisters born to wealth, raised to succeed, ready to love, destined to make waves.**

I've moved through life doing what's expected of me. I'm the middle daughter, the dutiful daughter. The one who braved a vicious attack and survived. The one who devoted herself to her family's business empire. The one who met an ambitious man and fell in love. We were going to run Fleur Cosmetics together, Zachary and I.

Until he got a promotion and left me in the dust. Maybe it's for the best, between his disloyalty and his wandering eye. But another man was waiting for me. Wanting me. He too has an overwhelming thirst for success, just like Zachary—perhaps even more so. He's also ruthless. And mysterious. I know nothing about Ryder McKay beyond that he makes me feel things I've never felt before.

One stolen moment, a kiss, a touch . . . and I'm hooked. Ryder's like a powerful drug, and I'm an addict who doesn't want to be cured. He tells me his intentions aren't pure, and I believe him. For once, I don't care. I'm willing to risk everything just to be with him. Including my heart. My soul.

My everything.

Advance praise for
Owning Violet

"*Owning Violet* owned me from the first page to the last. Ryder and Violet's chemistry is off the charts! Read it, own it, love it!"
        —*New York Times* **bestselling author Katy Evans**

Taking a deep breath, I slip my Chanel bag over my shoulder and exit the bathroom, stopping short when I see a man standing in the darkened hallway, almost as if he was waiting for me. His face is in shadows but I recognize his build, the way he holds himself. Confident, with that arrogant tilt of his head and those incredibly broad shoulders.

It's Ryder McKay.

"Well, well, well. Violet Fowler, how are you this evening?" His rumbly deep voice washes over me as he steps out of the shadows, tall and imposing and handsome as sin.

I take a step back, not wanting him in my personal space, but he invades it anyway. "Mr. McKay," I say politely, not daring to call him by his first name. That would imply I know him, that we're friends or at the very least friendly coworkers, and we're neither of those things. He may work at Fleur, but I rarely speak to him. I don't have to, and besides . . .

There's something about all that edgy darkness and how it radiates from him. He demands attention without saying a word, and there's an air of danger that surrounds him, that ensnares me despite my reluctance to be near him. The innate sexuality that he represents . . . it scares me.

He scares me.

"I've worked at Fleur long enough for you to call me Ryder, don't you think?" He pauses for a heavy beat and the air seems to fill with electricity as I wait for him to speak. "You don't mind that I call you Violet, do you?"

He somehow makes my name sound like a sexual promise. I take another step back and my butt hits the wall. He smiles, and I know *he* knows I've realized I'm trapped. "Of course you can call me Violet," I say, thankful my voice isn't shaking. I have no idea what to say to him, how to act. "Did you have a nice dinner?"

He grins. "Why yes, I did, thank you for asking. The view was spectacular." His gaze slides down the length of me, taking me all in. My breasts, my stomach, my hips, my legs, lingering on my feet before moving back up, his gaze once more on mine. "The food was good, too."

My cheeks heat, but it's not from the leftover tears. It's the way he looks at me, his gaze so bold, like he wants to devour me. His mention of the view is in reference to me. As if he's somehow attracted to *me*.

I don't believe it. He's just trying to unnerve me with his not-so-subtle flirting. And it's working.

"How's Zachary?" Ryder asks when I still haven't answered.

I jolt, giving myself a little shake. *Zachary.* I need to remember that my boyfriend is outside waiting for the car. Waiting for me. "Fine," I say as I step away from the wall. But that only brings me closer to Ryder and he doesn't budge. I can smell him. His scent is as dark and alluring as he is. "I should go. He's waiting—"

"I hear he's leaving for London." The expression on Ryder's handsome face is all polite sympathy, but with a hint of mockery in his dark blue eyes. He doesn't like Zachary and the feeling is mutual. Zachary complains about him all the time. I'm sure Ryder's thrilled that Zachary is leaving. "Trying out for a promotion, correct? I'm sure you're proud of him."

Proud of him? I should be. And seriously, did everyone know this bit of news but me? "H-how did you hear?" I press my lips together, angry that I let the little stutter slip. I need to remain composed, especially in the face of this particular man.

He's a shark. I know he takes advantage of the weak and gobbles them up. I've heard the stories. And those stories are more than half the reason Father is so pleased that he works at Fleur. Father admires a shark. It's why he loves Zachary so much, too, though Zachary is much smoother in his . . . predatory approach to business.

"My dinner partner told me the good news." He inclines his head when he notes my confusion. "I'm here with Pilar."

"Oh." Pilar. How could I forget? His relationship, his usual aloofness—it's all such a mystery. Hardly anyone knows much about him, but they all want to learn more. At the moment, though, he's being downright friendly with me.

"Yes." He smiles, and it's so dazzling I feel like I'm momentarily blinded. "Oh."

"How is Pilar?" I ask, being polite when I realize he seems to be waiting for a response. He still hasn't moved out of my way and I inhale discreetly, taking in his sharp, masculine scent. I let my gaze linger on him for a long moment as he looks down at the floor, as if he's savoring a personal joke. His eyelashes are long and thick, casting shadows upon his cheekbones, and my belly flutters when he glances up, his intense gaze meeting mine.

"She's well. Up to her usual tricks." The smile that curls the corners of his lips tells me he is in on the joke and I am definitely not. "I should probably go check on her."

"Where is she?"

"She's waiting at the front for her car. We rode together." His smile grows. "I wanted to come back here and check on you."

I frown. "Check on me?"

He shrugs those impossibly broad shoulders encased in fine Italian charcoal wool. "You seemed upset."

Really? Does that mean Zachary noticed too? He never said anything to me. I practically broke down in front of him at our table and he never uttered a word of concern.

"From the way you leapt up from the table, I had a feeling that Zachary just delivered the news." Ryder takes another step forward, reaching out to settle his big hand on my upper arm, giving it a brief, somewhat innocent squeeze.

My reaction to his touch is anything but innocent.

Available now:

ONE WEEK GIRLFRIEND
(One Week Girlfriend Quartet, Book 1)

Temporary. That's the word I'd use to describe my life right now. I'm temporarily working double shifts—at least until I can break free. I'm temporarily raising my little brother—since apparently our actual mother doesn't give a crap about either of us. And I always end up as nothing but the temporary girlfriend—the flavor of the week for every guy who's heard the rumor that I give it up so easily.

At least Drew Callahan, college football legend and local golden boy, is upfront about it. He needs someone to play the part of his girlfriend for one week. In exchange for cash. As if that's not weird enough, ever since he brought me into his world, nothing really makes sense. Everyone hates me. Everyone wants something from him. And yet the only thing Drew seems to want is . . . me.

I don't know what to believe anymore. Drew is sweet, sexy, and hiding way more secrets than I am. All I know is, I want to be there for him—permanently.

Chapter One

Drew [verb]: bring toward oneself, by inherent force or influence; attract.

I wait for her outside the bar, leaning against the rough brick building with my hands shoved deep inside my sweatshirt pockets, my shoulders hunched against the wind. It's cold as shit and dark from the clouds hanging low in the sky. No stars, no moon. Creepy, especially since I'm standing out here alone.

If it starts to rain and she's not done working, forget it. I'm leaving. I don't need this shit.

Panic sweeps through me and I take a deep breath. I can't leave and I know it. I need her. I don't even know her and she sure as hell doesn't know me, yet I need her to survive. I don't care if that sounds like I'm a complete pussy or what, it's true.

No way can I face next week on my own.

The music from within the tiny bar thumps loudly and I can hear everyone inside laughing and shouting. I swear I recognize more than a few voices. They're having a good time. Midterms are going down and the majority of us should be studying, right? Chilling in the library or bent over our desks, our heads in a book or hunched over our laptops, rereading notes, writing papers, whatever.

Most of my friends are in that bar drunk off their asses instead.

No one seems to care it's only Tuesday and there are still three more days left of testing and turning stuff in. It's make or break time, but everyone's focused on the fact that we're off next week. Most of us are hightailing it out of this shit small town where we go to college.

Like me. I'm outta here by Saturday afternoon. Though I don't want to leave. I'd rather stay here.

I can't.

She's off work at midnight. I asked one of the other waitresses who works at La Salle's when I snuck in there earlier, before anyone had really arrived. She'd been inside working, in the kitchen so she didn't see me. Which was fine.

I didn't want her to notice me. Not yet. And my so-called friends don't need to know what I'm up to either. No one knows about my plan. I'm afraid someone will talk me out of it if they did.

Like I have anyone to tell. It may look like I'm surrounded by plenty of people I call my friends, but I'm not close to any of them. I don't want to be. Getting too close to anyone only brings trouble.

The old wooden door swings open, creaking on its hinges, the noise from within coming at me like a physical blast as it smacks against my chest. She emerges into the darkness, the door slamming behind her, the sound echoing in the otherwise quiet night air. She's got on a puffy red coat that almost swallows her whole, making her legs covered in black tights look extra long.

Pushing away from the wall, I approach her. "Hey."

The wary glance she flicks in my direction says it all. "I'm not interested."

Huh? "But I didn't ask you anything."

"I know what you want." She starts walking and I fall in behind her. Chasing her really. I didn't plan on this. "You're all the same. Thinking you can wait around here, hoping to catch me. Trap me. My reputation is far more outrageous than what I've actually done with any of your friends," she tosses over her shoulder as she picks up speed. For such a little thing, she sure is fast.

Wait a minute. What she said, what's it supposed to mean? "I'm not looking for an easy mark."

She laughs but the sound is brittle. "You don't need to lie, Drew Callahan. I know what you want from me."

At least she knows who I am. I snag her arm just as she's about to cross the street, stopping her in her tracks and she turns to glare at me. My fingers tingle, even though all I'm grabbing at is coat fabric. "What do you think I want from you?"

"Sex." She spits the word out, her green eyes narrowed, her pale blonde hair glowing bright from the shine of the streetlight we're standing under. "Look, my feet are killing me and I'm exhausted. You chose the wrong night to think you can get with me."

I'm totally confused. She's talking like she's some sort of paid prostitute and I'm hoping to get a quickie blowjob in an alley or something.

Drinking in her features, my gaze settles on her mouth. She has a great one. Full, sexy lips, she could probably give a most excellent blowjob if I'm being honest with myself, but that's not why I'm here.

Makes me wonder exactly how many of my fellow teammates have got with her. I mean, the only reason I'm talking to her is because of that reputation she mentioned. But I'm not trying to buy her off for sex.

I'm trying to buy her off for protection.

About the Author

Monica Murphy is the New York Times and USA Today bestselling author of the One Week Girlfriend series. She writes new adult and contemporary romance for Bantam and Avon. She also writes romance as USA Today bestselling author Karen Erickson. A native Californian, she lives in the foothills below Yosemite.

Website: www.monicamurphyauthor.com
Facebook: www.facebook.com/MonicaMurphyAuthor
Twitter: www.twitter.com/MsMonicaMurphy
Email: missmonicamurphy@gmail.com

This paperback interior was designed and formatted by

E.M. TIPPETTS

BOOK DESIGNS

www.emtippettsbookdesigns.com

Artisan interiors for discerning authors and publishers.